SO-BSX-538

BOW DOWN, SHADRACH

JOY COWLEY

The Wright Group®

Bow Down, Shadrach

©Story by Joy Cowley
Cover illustration by Jim Hays
©1997 Wright Group Publishing, Inc.

All rights reserved. No part of this book may be reproduced or
transmitted in any form without written authorization from the
Wright Group permissions department.

The Wright Group
19201 120th Avenue NE
Bothell, WA 98011

Printed in the United States of America

10 9 8 7 6 5 4 3 2 1

ISBN: 0-7802-8307-4

This book is for all my young friends
who have taught me that it is never too
late to have a happy childhood.
Especially, it is for Sam Cowley
and Phoebe Glossop, who in a short
span of life left us a legacy of love.

CHAPTER ONE

They stopped halfway up the hill, and Hannah said to the new girl, "Do you want to see something really scary?"

"No," the new girl said.

"Well," said Hannah, "it's sort of scary if you're little like my brother Sky, but not for anyone our age. It's not far from here, just up the creek a bit. It's our secret, Mikey and Sky and me."

"I'd rather not go." The girl turned toward the creek and looked as though she was going to cry.

"It can't bite you or sting you or anything," said Hannah. "It's not that kind of scary." And she felt embarrassed that she didn't know the new girl's name.

"What is it?"

Hannah crossed her fingers before she spoke. "Hannibal Megosaurus."

The new girl didn't say anything. She looked at the creek and at Hannah, back and forth as though there were a line between the two.

"On the way back," said Hannah, "I'll show you our special horse, Shadrach. He's magic. He can do all sorts of tricks."

"Oh, all right," the girl said with a shrug.

They continued up the slope behind the house, following the line of trees beside the creek. The earth was stony and shared by patches of grass and fern and foxgloves in flower. Spears of color—pink, purple, white— moved in the wind that blew off the sea, and as they walked through the flowers, pollen stuck to their clothing.

On the other side of the foxgloves, they surprised a small flock of sheep with big lambs beside them. The ewes started, stared, and then rushed away with their lambs into the trees.

"They're a bit wild, aren't they?" the girl said.

"Sheep are always like that," said Hannah. "They have a courage in them people never see. They only pretend to be frightened. Would you like to pick some flowers?"

"Where?"

"Here." Hannah waved at the foxgloves.

The girl wrinkled her nose. "My father says foxgloves are weeds. He says they're poisonous."

Hannah filled up with a flood of feeling for the delicate flowers around them, each one a tiny cave of purple speckled with white. "Some are and some aren't," she said. "Anyway, we call them rabbit gloves."

"Why?" asked the girl.

"Because there aren't any foxes here in New Zealand."

The girl turned to walk on, but Hannah, eager to offer her something, called to her to look at the view. "You can see the whole bay from here."

The girl paused. "Yes, it's nice."

Hannah pointed. "There's Mikey! At the back of the house, feeding the chickens. I think Sky's inside." She raised her arm. "That's our mussel farm. See those black buoys halfway across the Sounds? And that's our boat on the mooring. If you look hard you'll see the winch for pulling in the mussel ropes."

"How can mussels make ropes?"

Hannah looked at the girl and breathed deeply the mixed smells of the sea and bush and sheep droppings. She was feeling strong. "Mussels don't make ropes. They grow on them. When they're big enough, we harvest them. I can drive the boat. Joe and Sophie let me."

"Who are Joe and Sophie?"

"My father and mother."

The girl laughed, her eyes looking as though they would cry. "You call your Mom and Dad Joe and Sophie?"

"No. My mother is Sophie. Joe is my father."

"That's very unusual. I couldn't call my parents by their names. If I went up to my father and said, 'Hi Basil!' he'd have a fit."

They both laughed at that, and Hannah said, "What's your name?"

"I thought you knew."

"I don't. At school, Mr. Gerritsen called you Ellie. Sophie said your name was Lana, and Mikey told me it was Anna. We had an argument about it."

"You're each partly right," the new girl said. "It's Eliana." And she spelled it for Hannah.

"That's very unusual," said Hannah, mimicking her voice, and they laughed again.

"Where's this magic pony?" Eliana asked.

"Horse," corrected Hannah. "Over that way. But first I'll show you—this other thing."

At the edge of the creek there was a thick stand of manuka trees, dark green and dusty and smelling like incense. The girls pushed under the branches, following a sheep path that led to the water.

The creek was not big, but it flowed swiftly, jumping from stone to stone, pool to pool, under an archway of branches. The banks on either side were high and loosely covered with dry leaves, but at the edge of the water the earth was still moist from spring flooding and green with ferns and moss, rich with its own wet smell.

The only sound down here was water music, and there was no movement except for the cool breath of the creek.

"We're close now," whispered Hannah. "When we get there, you can close your eyes if you want to, but you can't talk."

"Is it something dead?" Eliana asked.

Hannah didn't answer but crossed her fingers one on top of the other until her hands looked like the roots of trees.

"I don't like dead things," Eliana said.

"Shh!" responded Hannah.

Without sound, Hannah moved her lips to say "Apricots!" three times to build a wall of protection around her and Eliana. A few more steps along the edge of the stream, a short detour around a fallen log, and they were there.

In this place the creek fell down the slope like a straight curtain of white water, which was divided about halfway along by a rock the size of a dining table. The water splintered against the rock and then rushed around it, two fierce flows becoming one again on the other side. The rock, about three feet high, had almost straight sides and was covered with moss and small ferns that shivered and dripped with spray. Draped across the top of the rock, like a queen on a throne, was the great Hannibal Megosaurus.

"It's only the skeleton of a sheep!" said Eliana.

Shock went through Hannah. She thought, "Whoever shall speak aloud in the presence of Hannibal Megosaurus, verily all their food shall taste like mud for one week."

"You told me we were going to see a dinosaur!" Eliana stood on her toes. "How did a sheep get up there? Oh. I guess it fell down the bank and killed itself landing on the stone. Yuck! Its bones have turned green. How utterly gross!"

"Apricot, apricot, apricot!" Hannah chanted frantically in her head.

Eliana turned and started back the way they had come, flicking twigs and seeds off her sweatshirt. Hannah followed her up the bank, and when they were out of the trees and in open sunlight she said, "I did not tell you it was a dinosaur."

"What did you say then?"

"Hannibal Megosaurus! That's her name!"

"Her?" Eliana laughed. "Skeletons aren't him or her. If you think it's a her, why did you give it a masculine name like Hannibal?"

Hannah didn't know and didn't want to know.

"I suppose it's because Hannibal sounds like Hannah."

That thought had never occurred to Hannah. She was feeling cheated, her secret damaged. "Let's go back to the house," she said.

"What about the horse?" Eliana asked.

Hannah hesitated, feeling the same protective

instinct for Shadrach that she'd felt for the fox-gloves and now Hannibal Megosaurus. She wished she hadn't asked the new girl home, but Eliana had looked so helpless at school this morning, sitting there with her wet eyes and quietness. Hannah had felt sorry for her. It just went to show you could never tell with quiet people.

"All right. We'll go and see Shadrach."

They went along another sheep path that cut across the side of the hill and wound down to a little gully behind the house. They'd put Shadrach there last week because the grass was better than in his usual house paddock. The gully was the most fertile spot on the farm, and grass grew as thick as hair, with clumps of buttercups in the damp patches.

Hannah put her fingers in her mouth and whistled.

"Oh!" cried Eliana. "Show me how you do that!"

The moment was lost, however, for there was an immediate answer from under the trees, an eager noise whiffling through the nostrils and lips of the old draft horse as he came lumbering out in something between a trot and a hobble. He went immediately to Hannah and nuzzled her face, her hair. Hannah glanced back at Eliana and explained, "He's very, very old."

Eliana didn't speak. She simply looked, her mouth half-open.

Hannah hugged Shadrach's neck, filling herself with the smell of him and telling him fiercely that he was beautiful, beautiful. But at the same time, she could see him through Eliana's eyes: an old, arthritic horse with his ribs showing, a hairy, protruding lower lip hanging open, showing stumps of yellow teeth. She squinted her eyes. What was it about Eliana that made everything seem so ordinary?

"Did you say his name is Shadrach?" Eliana asked.

"Yes."

"That's in the Bible."

"I know."

"What about all these tricks he's supposed to do?"

"It's not a matter of suppose," cried Hannah. "He really does tricks. Years and years ago he belonged to a circus. There were three Clydesdale stallions, and their names were Shadrach, Meshach and—and—"

"Abednego," said Eliana.

"Yes. They were named after the three men in the story about the fiery furnace. These men wouldn't bow down to the statue of the king, so they got thrown into a huge bonfire."

"But they didn't get burned," said Eliana.

"The circus act was taken from that story. Joe told me about it. There was this man dressed up as a king, and he would say, 'Come to me, Shadrach. Come to me, Meshach. Come to me'—um—"

"Abednego."

"You know what would happen? The horses would walk backward away from him. Then he'd shout, 'Don't you walk away! Look me in the eye!' That's when the horses would turn their backs to him and flick their tails. Everyone laughed, Joe said. So then the king got really mad, and he yelled to each one of them, 'Bow down!' Every time he told them to bow down, they'd rear up on their hind legs. In the end, he got so angry he said they had to go into the fiery furnace."

"Not real fire!" said Eliana.

"Yes, real fire. There was a big burning hoop, and the stallions had to jump through it."

"How utterly cruel!" Eliana said.

Hannah smiled at her, warming to the emotion in her voice. She rubbed Shadrach's whiskery nose. "It was awful, that's for sure. Some circuses used to do terrible things to animals, Joe said. But the Society for the Prevention of Cruelty to Animals stopped the act, and the circus had to sell three Clydesdale horses who'd been trained to do the opposite of what they were told. You watch this." Hannah stepped back from Shadrach and said, "Look me in the eye!"

The old horse came forward and nudged at her hand for a piece of apple or a sugar cube.

"No, Shadrach!" Hannah stepped back again. "Look me in the eye!"

He paused like a stuck wind-up toy, then he sidestepped in a circle until his tail was presented to Hannah.

Eliana clapped her hands. "That's clever!"

Hannah went around Shadrach and kissed him on the nose. "Sophie and Joe bought him the year before I was born. That's how long we've had him. They thought he'd be good for a plow and cart, but Shadrach had other ideas. Joe says there was no way he could make him work. But he was really good with children. Only a year ago we were still riding him to school, Mikey and I. On the way home, if he got hot, he'd go into the sea with us on his back. But he's too old for riding now."

"Does he still remember the other circus tricks?" Eliana wanted to know.

"You bet he does. You're really magic, aren't you, Shadrach?"

"Can he still bow down?"

"Of course! He hasn't done it for ages, but he still remembers." Hannah stepped well away from him and called out loudly, "Bow down, Shadrach!"

He tossed his head a little and flicked his tail at the flies that settled on his flanks.

Sweat made his coat shine as though it had been oiled.

"Bow down, Shadrach!"

He knew the words. He whinnied, shuffled, and gathered energy for his response.

"Bow down, Shadrach!" Hannah shouted.

He seemed to be drawing strength into himself, tensing his muscles. His head went back, and then he was up, his great, hairy fetlocks pawing at the air, his hind legs shifting around in the grass. Up he stayed, his eyes rolling with the effort of it. Then suddenly he fell. Instead of coming down on all fours, he went sideways, his body hitting the ground. The sound was like that of a falling tree.

Neither Hannah nor Eliana moved.

Shadrach looked dead. His eye was turned so far back it showed only red. A muscle twitched in his leg, but apart from that he wasn't moving, wasn't breathing. Then, after a long time, there was a noisy pull of air into his lungs. He shuddered and gave another deep gasp.

Hannah got down on the ground and tried to lift his head. "Shadrach!"

He shuddered and twitched again. Then he tried to sit up, but his legs flailed uselessly as though he no longer knew what they were for, and he lay flat again.

Eliana said in her matter-of-fact way, "He probably broke his leg."

The words brought such a huge pain to Hannah that she couldn't speak. She knew that if it were true, Shadrach would have to be shot, and it would be her fault.

"Do you want me to go and get someone?" Eliana offered.

Hannah nodded, stroking Shadrach's muzzle. Then, as soon as Eliana was on her way to the house, Hannah started to cry.

Chapter Two

Sophie took Eliana home while Mikey and Sky scrubbed potatoes under the kitchen faucet, and Hannah stayed up in the gully helping Joe with Shadrach. At one point, Joe sent Hannah back to the house for the box of veterinary supplies, and Mikey saw that Hannah was crying, tears like snail tracks dried on her cheeks and more spilling out of her eyes. He wanted to tell her that Shadrach would be all right. He wanted to do one of his silly walks that would make her laugh. But his own throat thickened up, his eyes stung, and words got stuck. He couldn't even hug her, because his hands were wet from scrubbing potatoes.

Sky stared at her. "Why's Hannah crying? I won't cry when Shadrach gets deaded."

"Shadrach isn't getting deaded," said Mikey. "Finish that potato."

"It's finished. Can we have a funeral?"

"I can see some dirt on it."

"That's not dirt. That's a hole. Shadrach'd have a ginormous coffin. Bigger than Great-Grandpa's, right? Big as the boat, right?"

"If it's a hole, cut it out. Holes don't get in potatoes by themselves. You want to eat boiled potato worm?"

Sky dropped the potato quickly and wiped his hands on his shirt. "I'm going to see Shadrach."

When Mikey had finished the potatoes, he washed lettuce for salad. He was very interested in cooking. Last year, when he was eight, he won a dollar prize at the local fair for his shortbread, and Miss McNicol, the judge, said his shortbread was so good that she bought the whole tray from him for two dollars.

He read recipe books, finding exciting things to cook, like Chocolate Orange Gateau and Black Forest Cherry Cake and Bombe Alaska. But Sophie said cooking was like everything else— you had to start with the basics. Basic was a word for boring stuff like porridge, gravy, stew, custard. There were other restrictions, too. Since the time he had set fire to the curtain, Mikey wasn't allowed to use the stove when Sophie or Joe weren't there. Sometimes, though, they let him cook the whole dinner and dessert, and that meant he could sit back afterward while the others washed the dishes. Hannah and Sky moaned about all the pots and bowls he used.

He tore up the lettuce, drained it, and put it in a bowl with sliced tomatoes, cucumbers, scallions, and a lot of grated cheese on top. Mikey liked cheese.

He heard the car return, but Sophie didn't come into the house. He guessed that she had gone straight up to the gully to join the others with Shadrach. Mikey put the salad on the table and ran outside.

The sun was down behind the hills, and the whole bay was in cool shadow. The sun shone on the other side of the sound, but the hills there, too, were creased with dark shade.

Shadrach was still lying on his side, but his head was up. He was watching Joe, Sophie, Sky, and Hannah, who were sitting on the grass near him. Hannah looked pale, but she was no longer crying.

"Is his leg broken?" Mikey asked.

"No," said Joe. "No broken bones. It's not as bad as we first thought. We think he's just strained a ligament. We'll put a blanket on him, give him some hay, and he'll probably be up in the morning."

"I helped Joe give him a 'jection in the bum," Sky said.

"We gave him a shot to control the shock and give him a bit of energy," said Joe. "He's going to be okay. The main problem with him is age, and that's not something we can cure. He's definitely too old for tricks. I thought we would have all known that."

There was silence, and Mikey wanted to protest. He would never have made Shadrach bow down. But it was Joe's way of talking to include everyone, sharing the blame around the family rather than putting it on one person. At times it seemed unfair.

Sophie said, "Poor old Shadrach. The arthritis in his joints has gotten worse. I don't think he's going to manage another winter on this place."

"You said that last year," muttered Hannah. "He was all right."

"He wasn't all right, "Joe said. "He was in a great deal of pain, and I think it's high time we made a decision about his future."

"He'll be fine!" cried Hannah. "He'll live for years."

Mikey observed the panic in her face, and he sat down in the grass beside her. They all loved Shadrach, but love had lots of shapes and sizes, and while Mikey's love somehow fit in with cooking, playing chess, and his new fishing rod, for Hannah it was a people kind of love. Shadrach was as much Hannah's family as the rest of them were. Mikey had always known that.

Joe and Sophie looked at each other. They were holding hands. In front of them, Shadrach kept turning his head every now and then to be a part of the conversation. He'd twitch his ears and curl his oversized, hairy lips as though he had human words in his mouth and was trying to get them out. He was really old, Mikey thought. His eyes looked like Great-Grandpa's had looked. They were sunk deep with the whites turned red and the irises covered with a milky, blue film.

Joe said, "Shadrach shouldn't be here. The hills are steep. It's cold in winter. Sophie and I have been talking about it for some time and, well, we feel—"

"He'll have to go somewhere else," said Sophie.

"Where?" asked Hannah.

"Hey!" said Mikey. "We could take him around to Waitaria Bay. We'll ask Mr. and Mrs. Gerritsen if he can go in the school horse paddock. That's not steep."

"That's it!" cried Hannah. "Shadrach knows the school paddock, and he wouldn't be lonely, because we'd see him nearly every day."

"That's not what we had in mind, Hannah," said Sophie, reaching past Sky to stroke her daughter's hair. "It'd be nice for you, but what about Shadrach? It's cold in Waitaria Bay, too.

There's no shelter for him at night."

"We'll build him a stable," said Hannah.

"No, Shadrach is going to Nelson," said Joe.

"Nelson?" said Hannah.

"It's the practical thing to do," Joe said.

"Why Nelson?"

Joe held out his hand toward her. "Look, what do you think happens to horses when they have to be retired?"

"I know," said Mikey. "They go out to graze in clover."

Joe said, "Mikey, we don't have the money—"

"Yes, you're right, Mikey!" said Sophie, suddenly leaning forward. "Old horses are put into a beautiful paddock of red clover, and at night there are warm stables with oats and hay. They go to the Rest Home for Aged Equestrian Friends."

"Is that what it's called?" asked Hannah.

Sophie glanced at Joe. "Something like that. The stables are centrally heated in winter, and the horses get groomed every day. They have lots of people to love them."

"All right, Sophie," said Joe. "I don't think…"

Sophie put her hand on his arm and then said to Hannah, "You know we'll do absolutely the best thing for Shadrach."

"Won't it cost an awful lot?" asked Hannah. "You said we couldn't afford any extra."

"It won't cost a thing," Sophie said.

"How do we get him there?"

"Listen," said Joe. "A few days ago I had a phone call from Nigel Stack. He's going from Christchurch to Nelson with a horse trailer, and he wondered if I could meet him at Havelock with a couple of sacks of mussels. I've been thinking that he might be persuaded to make a detour and pick up Shadrach as well.

"Who's Nigel Stack?" asked Mikey.

"I remember him," said Hannah. "He works at some stables, and he really likes horses."

"He's crazy about them," Joe said. "You can be sure he'd see that Shadrach had a comfortable journey."

"Will his leg be better by then?" asked Hannah.

"He's almost ready to get up now," said Joe. "But what I'd do is make a sling for him and put it in the horse trailer to ease some of the weight off his legs." He stood up. "Who's going to help me get some hay for him?"

"I will," said Sophie. "Hannah, Mikey, Sky, you go in and set the table. Okay? And Hannah, I like your new friend Lana. She's lovely."

Hannah waited until her parents had moved out of earshot. Then she said, "Her name's not Lana, and she's not lovely. She's a murderess."

"Who did she murder?" asked Sky, immediately interested.

"She kills magic," said Hannah severely.

"What magic?"

"Say 'apricot'!"

"Apricot!" said Sky.

Hannah turned to Mikey.

He shrugged, put his hands in his pockets, and mumbled, "Apricot."

Hannah held her hands up as though she were catching air. "A-pri-cot!" she announced. Then she folded her arms, leaned forward, and whispered, "She spoke in the presence of H.M."

"Hannibal Megosaurus!" squeaked Sky, jumping up and down and holding on to the seat of his pants.

Hannah said in her storytelling voice, "With no regard for the sacred place, she criticized the powerful and splendorous H.M., who holds life and death in the palm of her hand."

"Palm of her hoof," corrected Sky.

Hannah crossed her fingers. "She actually sneered at Hannibal Megosaurus, and she said foxgloves were poisonous weeds. She's a barbarian."

"Did a calamity happen to her?" Sky asked eagerly.

"No, but it will."

Sky began to chant. "Her food will taste like dirt. Her food will taste like dirt."

"Mud," said Hannah. "For a whole week."

Mikey looked around them at the thick shadows brooding under the trees. "Come on,

Hannah. We made all that up."

"Of course we did," said Hannah, still in her storytelling voice. "When you make up something, it becomes real. It starts to live on its own, and there's no way you can unmake it."

"I thought Anna was okay," said Mikey. "She liked my posters."

"She has really big eyes," said Sky.

"Her name's not Anna or Lana," said Hannah. "It's Eliana." And she spelled it for them.

"Eliana," repeated Mikey. "That's not a very high-scoring Scrabble word."

Hannah stared at him, then laughed. "No, it isn't! Not as good as Hannah and Mikey and Sky."

One by one, they kissed Shadrach on the nose and said good night to him. They walked back to the house, Hannah going ahead of Mikey and Sky.

"What's a barbarian?" asked Sky.

"I don't know," Mikey said.

"I think it's a lady who does haircuts," said Sky. He stopped. "Does she cut people's hair?"

"Don't think so," said Mikey. "You'd better ask Hannah."

They caught up with Hannah and walked together down the path to the back door, entering the kitchen just in time to see the cat eating the cheese from the top of the salad.

Chapter Three

Sophie already had the dinghy halfway down the beach. "Bring the oars!" she yelled to Hannah.

"Can I row?" Hannah yelled back.

"I'll row out to the boat. When we get on board you can start it. Phew! This dinghy stinks. Have you kids left bait in it?"

"Sky caught a spottie, and it went under the seat. He couldn't get it out."

"He can try a bit of bent wire." Sophie steadied the dinghy while Hannah got in. "Do you know how to stop a fish from smelling?"

"Yeah," said Hannah, "you cut off its nose. Sophie, you told us that joke years ago."

Sophie laughed and, settling herself in the bow, picked up the oars. A rush of herring swam away from the boat and plopped some distance away, making circles on the dark green water.

The oars creaked and splashed, creaked and splashed, and in all that calm their wake spread out behind them as a straight path edged with bubbles. When they neared the mooring, Hannah reached out to grab the ladder of the mussel boat, and a moment later they were both on board, the dinghy tied up to the mooring buoy.

Hannah knew how to start the diesel engine. Joe had shown her many times. But Sophie still hovered anxiously as Hannah backed the boat away from the moored dinghy and then put it in forward gear. Too short to see over the wheel, Hannah had to stand on an old nail box that Joe had put in the boat for her.

When they got to the mussel farm, Sophie took over and coasted alongside the first row of mussel buoys that bobbed in the water like a row of black plastic drums. Beads for a giant's necklace, Sky used to call them. Hannah watched as her mother lowered the grappling iron. Then she blocked her ears to the screeching of the winch as the rope, with its heavy encrustation of green and black shellfish, came out of the water and over the side of the boat.

The mussels were a good size for eating, as long as the palm of Hannah's hand. They were stuck together, bound by the fibers of their beards, and had to be separated before being put into a sack. Hannah held one close to her face, secretly admiring the beauty that was always revealed when something was really looked at. Hannah couldn't understand anyone who didn't believe in magic. Everything was magic. Every single thing. It was just a matter of looking. The more a thing was looked at, the more it would go beyond itself into the mysterious world that moved at the corner of one's eye. Like mussels. Mussels were the voices of the sea. The shells opened like mouths taking in and giving out all the secrets of the tides. When you ate mussels, you filled yourself with the sea's secrets, whether you were aware of it or not.

"You don't have to separate each one," said Sophie. She had dropped the mussel ropes over the side and was now pushing Hannah's box away so that she could move the boat. "Nigel can do that. Just break them up into clumps small enough to get into the sacks."

But Hannah took her time over the mussels. She felt that if she cleaned and separated them for Nigel Stack, he would take extra good care of Shadrach, although another part of her thinking told her that life didn't work that way. Hannah sighed. For all her love of ritual and magic, there was a voice in her that sounded very much like the voice of Eliana Grouse, a voice that killed magic and then accused her of superstition.

Back at the mooring, Sophie and Hannah lowered the sacks of mussels into the dinghy and got in themselves.

"That stinking fish again!" cried Sophie. "I hope it doesn't spoil Nigel's mussels. I've told Mikey and Sky to leave the dinghy clean after they go fishing."

"I like fishing, too," said Hannah. "Why don't I have a new rod and reel like Mikey's?"

"No reason," said Sophie. "Only you chose to spend your money on some new shoes."

"I have enough now for a rod."

"Fine. You know what to do. Put it on the list, and we'll get it for you next time we're in town."

Hannah said as though she had just thought of it, "Hey! We could have a day off school next week and go to Nelson. There's a good fishing shop there."

Sophie shook her head. "We've already talked about that."

"But Sophie, he'll be homesick! I just want to make sure they're looking after him."

"Stop worrying about Shadrach. He'll be very well looked after, I promise you. Do you want some good news?"

"How good?"

"On a scale of one to ten, I'd say ten and a half."

"What?"

"When the lambs are sold, we're going to buy a pony. You can choose it."

Hannah was silent.

"I thought you'd be all excited," said Sophie.

Hannah struggled with tears and overcame them by anger. "Shadrach hasn't even gone yet, and you're trying to replace him!"

Sophie looked at her for a moment, then said, "We'll talk about it later."

They put the sacks of mussels on the tractor and took them up to the house. Joe was in the garage finishing the rope and canvas sling he'd made for Shadrach's journey to Nelson. Sky and Mikey were with him, hammering something from an old wooden box.

"Nigel phoned," Joe called to Sophie. "He should be here any moment."

So soon! Hannah turned and ran through the gate at the back of the house, up and over the fold of the hill to the gully where Shadrach was grazing head down among the buttercups. She stopped and put two fingers in her mouth.

He answered her whistle immediately.

"Darling Shadrach!" she called.

He'd been slow enough before his fall, but now he moved like a big tortoise, feeling each leg before he put weight on it. Even when his four hooves were firm on the ground, his legs would quiver, the movement going all the way up to the bones hunched under the skin on his back.

Still, his welcome was as strong as ever as he nickered and dribbled saliva over Hannah's hair.

"You'll feel better there," Hannah told him. "You'll be warm, and there'll be other horses for company. Lots of red clover, too. Sophie said all the people that work there are kind, and you'll get lots of love." She stopped at that, hating the thought of someone else loving Shadrach as much as she did. She put her arms around his neck. "I promise you, Shadrach, I'll never get a pony. Not as long as I live."

In the distance she heard a crunch of gravel as a car came around the point of the bay. Each time she'd heard that sound, she'd waited for the vehicle to pass in a cloud of dust and disappear around the headland. This car didn't keep going. The dust cloud stopped at their driveway. Hannah pushed her face into Shadrach's mane, remembering all the times she'd ridden him with her head against his neck. "I'll come and see you often. I'll bring you some apples when they get ripe."

"Hannah! Hannah! The trailer is here!"

She saw Mikey running over the ridge, squinting his eyes against the sun. "Hannah? Joe said you have to bring Shadrach down to the house."

Nigel Stack had once been a jockey. He still walked like one, shoulders forward, with wide, springy steps. Hannah didn't know his age, for although he was bald and wrinkled, he talked and acted like a young man. He had a rusty, cream-colored station wagon caked with dust and a double horse trailer.

"You didn't tell me it was a dirt road," he said to Joe. "Man, I've been eating so much dust my guts'd grow a tree."

"You'll have some lunch with us," Joe laughed.

"Thanks, but no thanks. A cup of tea and I'll be away. It's been a slow trip, and I have to get back to Nelson this afternoon." He unbolted the doors at the back of the trailer. "We'll get Lacemaker out and give her some water."

"You have a horse in there already?" asked Hannah.

"Sure, sure! Why'd you think I was on the road, giving the trailer some exercise? Whoa, girl! Easy, easy!" He had opened the door to a beautiful thoroughbred that was twitching nervously and shifting her hooves in a rapid tap dance. "You're all right, girl. Say, anyone got a bucket of fresh water?"

Joe went to get water. Mikey, Hannah, and Sky stood at the door of the trailer, trying to see the horse.

"Out of the way!" said Nigel. As he backed Lacemaker down the ramp, Hannah reached out and tried to touch her. She shied away, almost stumbling on the boards. "Don't do that!" Nigel yelled at Hannah. "Anything happens to this champion, I lose my job—and my head! Hey, hey girl! Steady, pretty one!" Nigel then tried to soothe the horse and Hannah at the same time. "It's not your fault, Hannah lass. She's in a flighty mood. Where's your pony?"

"By the house," said Hannah. "He's not a pony. He's a Clydesdale."

"Clydesdale?"

"Yes."

"A bloomin' big draft horse?"

"That's right."

Nigel swore and wiped his hand over his bald head. "That's all I need. I can't take a draft horse on that road. Not with her. I'll break an axle."

Hannah almost smiled. "He is really heavy."

Joe was coming back with the water, Sophie beside him. Nigel called to him. "Hey, you didn't tell me I was taking a big plow horse. No way, Joe! I can't do it!"

Joe said, "Hannah, bring Shadrach."

Hannah went around the house to where Shadrach was standing patiently, the end of his rope halter trailing on the ground. She picked it up so that he wouldn't trip over it, but she didn't need to lead him. He followed her unbidden, pleased to see her again.

When Nigel looked at Shadrach, his face opened with surprise. "That's not a horse!" he said. "That's a famine-struck camel!"

"We told you he was old," Sophie said.

"You said old, but he's prehistoric! He's not going to last the trip!"

"You'd be surprised at how strong he is," said Joe. "I've made a sling for him. And don't worry about the trailer. As you can see, he doesn't weigh all that much."

"What if his heart gives out?" Nigel asked.

"His heart's okay," Joe assured him. "Honestly, he's much better than he looks."

"What a load!" Nigel said. "Lacemaker and Pacemaker!"

They put Shadrach in the trailer first. Then Joe rigged up the sling under him. The old horse accepted it all without any kind of protest, as though this happened to him every day. When Joe had finished, Nigel brought Lacemaker back to the ramp. The beautiful racehorse, with her sleek coat and bobbed tail, sniffed at Shadrach and went up the ramp with a quick whinny of welcome. In the trailer she put her head across and huffed in his ear.

Hannah was pleased. Nigel's comments had made her angry and left her without confidence in the man's reputation for being good with horses. But at least Lacemaker had recognized Shadrach for the fine horse he was and was making every effort to be friendly. She'd be a good traveling companion for him.

The sacks of mussels, still dripping, were put on a plastic sheet in the trunk of Nigel's car.

Then they all went into the house, where Mikey had set out a plate of his special shortbread for morning tea.

Nigel, who had known Joe for years, talked about old times and the friends they both knew. Joe made interested noises, but the whole family was under the weight of a silence. Whatever the topic of conversation, thoughts kept drifting back to Shadrach waiting in the horse trailer. Hannah saw her father's eyes looking into space beyond Nigel's head, and she observed Sophie breaking a piece of shortbread into crumbs, without purpose. Even Sky was quiet, and Sky usually stopped talking only when he was sick or asleep.

Hannah looked at Joe. "When are we going to Nelson to see Shadrach?"

"What?" said Nigel Stack. He looked quickly at Joe and then said, "Oh, yeah. Sure."

"We'll talk about that later," Joe said to Hannah. Then to Nigel he said, "Want more tea?"

"No thanks." Nigel stood up. "I have to go. If my boss ever finds out I came all this way to pick up an old horse, I'll be taking a long walk down a short jetty. Thanks for the mussels. They'll be a treat."

Hannah had decided she wouldn't watch the horse trailer leave, but when the time came she was there with the rest of the family.

Mikey stood beside her. "We're making a sled for the hill. When it's finished you can have a ride."

Hannah sniffed and nodded.

Nigel Stack was driving very slowly over the bumps in the driveway, which was a good thing, and Shadrach was with Lacemaker, who liked him. But what would it be like at the other end? Were the horses just as friendly at the Rest Home for Aged Equestrian Friends, and were the stables really as warm and luxurious as Sophie said? How could Sophie be so sure?

Hannah stopped waving. In a bold movement and without any kind of protection, she folded her arms and thought the words, "Oh Hannibal Megosaurus, mighty spirit of the animals of this bay, I command you to go with Shadrach and protect him from all troubles."

Joe put his arm around Hannah's shoulders. "Did Sophie tell you we're going to get a pony?"

"I don't want a pony! Never!"

"Never is a long time," said Joe.

The car and horse trailer were out of sight, but a column of dust rose from the road and flowed toward them, thick as smoke.

"We'll talk about it again in a few months," said Joe.

Shaking her head, Hannah pulled away. Then she went to the gully to cry.

Chapter Four

That evening, Joe found Sophie standing out-side the children's bedroom, her hand resting lightly on the doorknob. He was going to say something, but she put her finger on her lips, and he walked to the living room. Minutes later, she came back, saying in a hushed voice, "I've been listening to a story."

"One of Hannah's?" he asked.

"One of Hannah's." She sat down at her spin-ning wheel, picking up some combed wool that would eventually become Joe's pullover for the next winter. "It was a weird story about some giant ewe with a fleece six feet long, made of silver clouds." She spread the wool in her hands and laughed. "Imagine spinning a yarn like that."

"Did the ewe have some name like Hannibal Brontosaurus?" asked Joe.

"You've heard the story?"

"Not from Hannah. Sky fills me in from time to time. It's ongoing—a fairy tale soap opera.

She's constructed a sort of mythology around the skeleton of that old ewe lying on the rock in the creek."

"It sounded crazy," said Sophie. "I worry about that child. I used to think she'd grow out of her wild imagination, but it seems to be getting wilder as she gets older."

"It's born in her," said Joe. "Your Scottish mother and my Maori grandmother were both women of creative power. The two streams have converged in Hannah. I hope we do the right things to encourage it."

"Encourage it!" Sophie fed yarn into her bobbin, her foot working the treadle, clack, clack, clack. "She lives in a world of superstition!"

"Well, most people have a certain amount of superstition in them," Joe said easily. "I always reckon that superstition holds the seeds for inner growth."

"It can go the other way," Sophie said. "One day a psychiatrist might be labeling it schizophrenia or paranoia."

Joe, who had himself inherited much from his grandmother, laughed. "Labels belong to the people who use them. Hannah's a healthy little girl with a wonderful imagination, and if this world needs anything, it's imagination."

Sophie's spinning slowed. "In her story tonight, this giant sheep was going on a journey with an old horse. When the horse got tired, the sheep carried him. When the horse was hungry, the sheep fed him. At the end, the horse got so old he was going to die. The sheep wrapped him in a rainbow and made him young again."

"That's beautiful," said Joe, "And it tears me up inside. I know how much she loves Shadrach. I felt terrible when I saw him walk into the trailer like that—complete trust. I wanted to take him out again and give him the dignity of death and burial on this place."

The spinning wheel stopped. "Joe, she keeps nagging about a trip to Nelson to see him."

"I know." Joe put the combed wool in the basket beside her. He was about to take some more fleece from the sack when the phone rang in the kitchen. "I'll get it," he said.

He left the door open, and above the clatter of the wheel Sophie heard isolated phrases. Joe was very concerned about something, and the words "sorry" and "bad luck" came through to her. Then she heard the name "Nigel." She thought that Shadrach had died somewhere on the journey.

Poor old Shadrach. Tears came to her eyes. Of all the family, she was probably the least attached to the old horse, but because they'd bought him soon after their marriage, he was a part of what she and Joe had created together. Moving to the bay, clearing scrub and thistles, fencing land, establishing gardens, building sheds, having babies, one season of fruitfulness flowing into another, and Shadrach had always been there. He was so gentle, the quietest stallion they'd ever known, and perhaps the ugliest, with his huge head and over-developed mouth. He was better suited to a freak show than a circus, someone remarked when they got him. He was a "people" horse, especially good with children. She thought of all the times he'd opened the bar of the gate with his teeth and then gone around to the children's bedroom window. When Hannah was only four, she would climb out the window directly onto his back, no saddle or reins.

Sophie stopped spinning and got up for a tissue. She was blowing her nose when Joe came back.

"That was Nigel. Guess what?"

She couldn't say anything.

"He did break an axle, after all."

"A broken axle?"

"Yes. On the trailer."

"Shadrach's all right?" she asked.

"Okay, I think. The horses are in a holding paddock for the night, and the trailer's up on a jack. Nigel's in Havelock making phone calls, wanting to know what he should do to keep the mussels fresh. I told him to keep them wet."

"Can they fix it?"

"There's a new part coming from Nelson in

the morning, and he'll be leaving by lunchtime, he says. His main problem is that he's worried about his boss. He'll lose his job if the boss finds out he came here to pick up Shadrach."

"Poor Nigel! Did he say how it happened?"

"On a rough patch of road near Linkwater." Joe rubbed the side of his neck. "I feel bad about it. He said he'd break an axle, and I assured him he wouldn't."

"Is he going to take Shadrach the rest of the way?"

"Yes, he said he would. The road from Linkwater to Nelson's in good shape."

Sophie said, "If his boss did find out, maybe we could pay for Nigel's time and the damage to the trailer."

"That's not the problem," said Joe. "It's Lacemaker. Taking her anywhere is like having the queen on board. You don't make detours with royalty. Imagine if they'd gone over a bank with Lacemaker!"

"Thank goodness they didn't," said Sophie.

"Hey, are you all right?" Joe was looking closely at her.

She laughed softly. "When I heard you on the phone, I thought Shadrach was dead. Silly, wasn't it?" Then she said, "We won't tell the children about this."

"No," he replied. "The less said on the subject of Shadrach, the better."

Sophie started spinning again. "Before the phone rang, we were talking about Hannah. She keeps asking about a trip to Nelson to see him."

"Yes, and she won't give up."

"We'll have to tell her something."

"Wait a few days," said Joe. "Then we'll tell them all that Shadrach has died."

CHAPTER FIVE

The school at Waitaria Bay was small: two rooms, two teachers, and twenty-nine children from thirteen years old down to Sky, who was a new entrant at five years and one month old.

Mikey thought it was the best school ever, although he had never been to another school to make a comparison. Mr. Gerritsen was the head of the school "family." He taught all the usual things, plus lessons on catching eels, raising orphaned lambs, skinning opossums, and building bush huts. The school was well-situated for such activities, right on the sea with a stream nearby and bush-covered hills behind it.

Until the year before, Mikey had ridden to school with Hannah on Shadrach. Shadrach would then spend the rest of the school day grazing in the horse paddock behind the classrooms. Now they caught the school bus driven every morning by Mrs. Gerritsen, who much preferred riding horses.

When she stopped for them the morning after Shadrach had gone, she said, "I'm sorry to hear about dear old Shadrach."

"He's in a better place," said Mikey. "His arthritis was getting very bad."

Mrs. Gerritsen glanced at Hannah, then said, "Yes, I'm sure it's for the best."

At school, it seemed that everyone knew about the horse trailer taking Shadrach away. News traveled fast in a small community, but it wasn't always accurate. Two girls, Kirsty Jones and Debbie Taylor, had heard that Shadrach had been killed for dog food.

Mikey laughed. "No way! He's gone to this place where they look after old horses. It's like an old people's home. They treat them really great."

Kirsty's face lit up with relief. "Just wait till I tell those other kids," she said and ran off.

At the afternoon break, Eliana Grouse sat beside him. "Hello, Michael."

"Hello." He was still shy about pronouncing her name.

"Your sister hardly talks to me," Eliana said. "Have I done something wrong?"

Mikey shook his head. "It's Shadrach. He was extra special to Hannah. She doesn't want to talk to anyone right now."

"Poor Hannah. Well, at least Shadrach's had a stay of execution."

"What do you mean?"

"Didn't you know that the horse trailer broke down?"

"No."

"The man who took Shadrach away didn't get past Linkwater."

"Who told you that?"

"I found out from Mom at lunchtime. She called your mother this morning and your mother told her. I think it was a broken axle. The trailer was being fixed this morning, and they were going on to Nelson this afternoon."

"Sophie told your mother all that?"

"That's right. Mom said your father got a call from the man last night."

"They didn't tell us," said Mikey.

"Oh. Well, they probably didn't want to upset Hannah," Eliana said.

Mikey stared hard at her to see if she was telling the truth. Her eyes were wide and shining, and her face showed nothing but concern. If she was lying, she was very good at it. He said, "What do you mean by a stay of execution?"

"I don't know. I just said it. I suppose 'execution' sounded better than 'killed.'"

"He isn't getting killed," said Mikey. "That rumor's wrong. He's gone to a place called the Rest Home for Aged Equestrian Friends."

Eliana laughed quickly and put her hand over her mouth to stop it. "That's a funny name for a dog food factory."

"He hasn't gone to a dog food factory!"

"Yes, he has."

"No!" He shook his head. "They are stables especially for old horses."

Eliana said, "It's the Wuff Stuff Dog Food Company. Michael, I know. The other day when your mother took me home from your place, she got the address and phone number from my parents. Dad gets all our dog food wholesale from Wuff Stuff. The man pays thirty dollars each for old horses, and your mother said she was going to put the money toward a new pony for the children."

"It's not true," said Mikey, but in a quiet voice.

"If they said something different, it's because they're trying to spare your feelings. Michael, don't let them know I told you this."

"But they wouldn't send Shadrach to a dog food factory!" cried Mikey. "I just know they wouldn't! It'd be like sending Great-Grandpa away to be killed."

"I'm sorry, Michael," said Eliana. "Perhaps I shouldn't have mentioned it. But everyone else knows."

"Is this dog food factory in Nelson?"

"On the other side of the city—on Harvey Road." Eliana put her hand on Mikey's arm for a second, then stood up. "Don't worry about him, Michael. It'll be quick. He won't feel a thing."

The bell rang almost immediately, and there wasn't time to talk to Hannah. But in class, while they were supposed to be working on a project about volcanoes, Mikey wrote a long letter to Hannah and passed it to her. He watched his sister read it and felt her pain as he saw her shoulders become rigid and her face go white.

Mr. Gerritsen saw it, too. He said, "Hannah, have you got something there you want to share with the rest of us?"

Hannah shook her head and didn't look at him.

"Do you want to share it with me?" Mr. Gerritsen said, holding out his hand.

Hannah passed him the note.

He read it silently, then said in a kind voice, "Hannah, would you like to be excused for a few minutes? Mikey, you can go out with Hannah if you like. The rest of us are going back to work. Come on, everyone. What are the names of two active New Zealand volcanoes?"

Hannah and Mikey sat in the sun, in front of the school. It was a still afternoon with the air full of the noise of nesting birds. The sea was busy, too: water splashing and white terns fluttering above it like scraps of paper. There'd be a shoal of kahawai out there, Mikey thought. He liked the way Sophie cooked kahawai with onions and coconut cream.

45

Hannah, who had been knotted up in silence for a long time, said, "It's true."

"How do you know?"

"Of course it's true! They wouldn't say what the place was exactly called. They wouldn't say exactly where it was. I asked when we could go and see Shadrach. They wouldn't give an answer. They're so vague about everything!"

"What about the horse trailer breaking down? Do you think that's true, too?"

"The phone did ring last night," Hannah said. "Joe answered it, but I couldn't hear what he was saying."

To comfort her, Mikey said, "I think we should get Shadrach back."

"How do we do that?"

"Tell Joe and Sophie we know all about it and we want him home again."

"You think that'd work?"

"No," he admitted.

"So what's another brilliant idea?"

"Well, we could call the man at the Wuff Stuff Dog Food place and say there's been a mistake. We'd ask him to put Shadrach on a horse trailer and send him home to us."

"Where would we get a horse trailer, and who would pay for it?"

Mikey was struggling with the enormity of the problem. "How much would a trailer cost?"

"Hundreds and hundreds—unless you know someone who owns one."

"We could find one somewhere," Mikey persisted.

"And while we're spending days searching for someone with a horse trailer who'll bring him back for nothing, what happens to Shadrach?"

Mikey gave up. "I dunno."

"If we're going to do something, it has to be tommorow," said Hannah. "Let's go to Nelson in the morning—just you and me."

"What will Sophie and Joe say?"

"They won't know. No one will know until it's too late. There's a freight truck from Transport Nelson coming in tomorrow early. It's bringing the lumber for the Taylors' new house. We'll get a ride back with it."

"And not go to school?"

"Obviously."

"The driver won't give us a ride. What are we going to tell him?"

"Nothing. We'll get up on the back and hide under the cover. He won't even know we're there. When we get to Nelson, we'll go straight to the dog food factory. We'll tell the man it was a mistake, and we'll take Shadrach back. Then we'll call Joe and Sophie, and they'll have to find a way of getting us all back."

"But you reckoned they wouldn't bring him back."

47

"They'll have to!" hissed Hannah. "We won't leave him. If they want us, they have to take Shadrach as well."

Mikey rubbed his arms. He was a peaceful person, and talk of rebellion made him uncomfortable, as though there was a deep itch under his skin. He didn't want to go to Nelson, but he couldn't let Hannah do it on her own.

"Don't worry," said Hannah. "I've got it all worked out."

"But Shadrach might be already dead when we get there."

She turned on him. "Mikey, you are so stupid! Of course he won't be dead!"

He wanted to ask her why not, but didn't.

"We'd better go back inside," Hannah said in a calmer voice. She smiled and put her arm around his shoulder. "You're not really stupid, Mikey. You're not even a little bit stupid. It's just that nothing can happen to Shadrach, because H.M. is looking after him."

Mikey said, "Well, I hope that Wuff Stuff man believes in your fantastic Hannibal Megosaurus."

"It doesn't matter what he believes. As long as you and I believe, it'll be true. You have to believe, Mikey, with all your heart and mind and soul and lungs and liver—"

"Okay," said Mikey, "I believe it. Apricot, apricot, apricot." And together they went back to their classroom and volcanoes.

After school, in the few minutes before the bus, Mikey saw Hannah talking to Eliana Grouse, their heads so close they were almost touching. Then he saw her with Debbie Taylor, and he guessed she was finding out more about the freight truck. He felt a deep unrest in his stomach.

Neither he nor Hannah mentioned Shadrach when they got home. Sophie and Joe were working in the garden, Joe making late spring plantings of lettuce and beans, and Sophie repairing the netting that would protect the strawberries from birds and opossums. Joe and Sophie didn't talk much about Shadrach, either, but Sky did.

"I bet Shadrach likes that place a lot. I bet they give him so much to eat he gets fat, fat, fat." And he tried to imitate the walk of a fat horse.

"Put your schoolbag away, Sky," Sophie said. "There's some cold juice in the fridge if you want it."

During supper, Joe said to Mikey and Hannah, "You two are very quiet. What are you thinking about?"

"Shadrach," said Mikey.

Hannah turned quickly in her chair and stared at him.

"What about Shadrach?" asked Joe.

"I was just wondering how he is."

Before Joe could say anything, Sophie put her hand on his arm. "Shadrach's fine," she said. "He's never had it so good."

Mikey expected Hannah to jump out of her chair, shout, or cry. He thought she might bring it all out in the open and save them a lot of trouble. But she didn't. She simply sat there eating, not saying a word.

CHAPTER SIX

Hannah could barely look at her parents. She was feeling bruised inside, too sore for words, and she avoided talking to them. She went to bed early and the next morning was first up. She woke a reluctant Mikey and ordered him to the window to watch the road for the freight truck. Then she packed her schoolbag for the trip to Nelson. She opened the box containing her savings and counted out thirty dollars plus another five.

"That's a lot of money," said Mikey. "We're not going shopping."

"We might have to buy back Shadrach. Thirty dollars, Eliana said."

"The man might just give him back," Mikey suggested.

"He might," Hannah said grudgingly. "But I'll bet people who kill horses and cut them up for dog food don't give away anything."

"Dogs have to eat, too," said Mikey.

"They don't have to eat horses! I told you to stay at that window!"

"Grump, grump, grump," said Mikey, and he went back to watch for the truck. It wasn't seven yet, and the day still had a newborn look, everything wet with the dew and the sun pale yellow on the bay. There was no tell-tale cloud of dust on the other side of the water.

Having stowed the money in the bottom of her bag, Hannah then got an empty cardboard box and put several stones wrapped in tissue paper into it.

"What's that for?" asked Mikey.

"Bait."

"Huh?"

"For the truck driver." Now Hannah was putting on the lid and covering the box with red gift wrap. "We're putting a present on the road to make him stop. You could lie down on the road instead. But he might not stop in time. Anyway, if you were on the road you wouldn't be able to hide on the back with me." She tied silver ribbon around the red paper. "Mikey— window!"

"I know, I know," he said, turning back to the road.

In the lower bunk, Sky groaned and rolled over to face them, blinking into wakefulness. Hannah quickly thrust the wrapped box into her bag.

She smiled at her younger brother and chanted the rhyme he himself had made up. "Hi, Sky! How high? In the sky, five miles high."

Sky's eyes snapped open. "I'm not going to be Sky today."

"He's going to change his name again," said Mikey. Then Mikey did one of his funny walks around the bedroom, clutching his heart and saying, "Help! Help! I feel a change of name coming on!"

"What are you going to be called?" Hannah asked.

"Boomy-boomy-nutcake."

"That's a name?"

Sky solemnly nodded.

Mikey changed his walk to a high-stepping march and beat an imaginary drum. "Boomy-boomy-nutcake! Boomy-boomy-nutcake!"

"Window!" yelled Hannah.

He saluted, did a quick turn, and leaned over the sill. "Not in sight, sir!"

"What's not in sight?" asked Sky.

At that moment, Sophie put her head around the door. "You two up already? Great! Come on, Sky. Hit the floor!"

"I'm not Sky. I'm Boomy-boomy-nutcake."

"That's his name for the day," said Mikey.

Sophie laughed. "Nutcase, more like it. I just want to announce that breakfast's ready when you are. What are you looking at, Mikey?"

"The freight truck," said Mikey, pointing to the billowing dust that flowed into the bay.

Sophie stood with him at the window as the dust came nearer, boiling in the air, and they could see the truck with its large load laced under a canvas cover. "That must be the lumber for the Taylors' house," Sophie said. "Close the window before the dust comes in." She glanced at Sky on the way out. "Out of bed, Boomy-boomy-nutcase, or I'll tickle your feet."

Hannah felt relief when Sophie went out of the room. Her head was full of Sophie's words—red clover, heated stables, lots of loving attention—and there was an ache in her chest that made breathing difficult. She didn't think she could trust Sophie in anything, ever again.

As soon as breakfast was over, she was anxious to leave. She didn't know how long it would take the driver to unload the freight truck but guessed he could be coming back even earlier than the school bus. She put Mikey's and Sky's lunches in their bags and hurried them out the door, talking to Mikey in whispers, which made Sky resentful.

"You got secrets," he said. He called out. "Sophie? Mikey and Hannah got secrets, and they won't tell me!"

They rushed him quickly down the driveway, with an avalanche of reassuring words. Mikey looked at Hannah and said, "What about him?"

Hannah glumly considered her youngest brother. She had planned every detail of the freight truck ride to Nelson but had forgotten all about Sky.

He knew they were up to something. "This isn't where we wait for the bus," he said. "Why don't we go to the other place?"

Hannah didn't want to tell him that the usual waiting place could be seen from the house, whereas this was well concealed by a clump of trees She said, "Listen, Sky…"

He turned away and shut his eyes.

"Sorry, Boomy-boomy-nutcake. Mikey and I aren't going to school today. You'll have to get the bus by yourself."

"Where are you going?"

"To Nelson," said Mikey. "To get Shadrach."

Hannah glared at him. Mikey always blurted too much.

"I'm going, too," said Sky.

"You can't," said Hannah. "It's hard and dangerous. You have to go to school as usual."

Sky was looking from one to the other. "Why are you getting Shadrach?"

So then they had to tell him, quickly, urgently, one eye on the road for the sign of dust, which could mean school bus or freight truck.

"I'm coming with you!" said Sky, jumping up and down and clutching the seat of his pants. "I am! I am so!"

Hannah looked helplessly at Mikey, who shrugged and said, "As soon as he gets on the school bus, Mrs. Gerritsen is going to ask him where we are."

"I'll tell!" Sky said triumphantly.

"All right," said Hannah. "You can come, too."

Mikey and Sky stood in the grass at the edge of the road while Hannah climbed up the bank to a place where she could see the whole bay. The sun was already hot, and a fine film of dust covered the bush and tree ferns.

Sky was picking up stones and throwing them down into the sea on the other side of the road. Mikey didn't join him. Hannah could tell from his scrunched-up look that he was unhappy.

The school bus came down the road first.

"Hide!" cried Hannah. The other two came scrambling up the bank beside her, and they all pressed back among the manuka and tree fern.

The small, red bus, covered with dust, slowed down near their usual waiting place, then stopped. Hannah held her breath. She had expected it to drive past, but the bus waited there, busy with arms and legs and voices. Mrs. Gerritsen looked up toward the house. She honked once, twice.

"Apricot!" Hannah breathed. "Apricot! Apricot!"

Neither Joe nor Sophie came out of the house. Mrs. Gerritsen honked again, and the bus moved away.

The dust had barely settled when a new cloud appeared, and they heard the distinctive rumbling of the freight truck. Quickly, Hannah dived down the bank with the red-wrapped box and placed it in the middle of the road. She climbed back up the bank. "We should be able to jump from here—right onto the back of the truck. We'll have plenty of time. It'll take him a while to unwrap those stones."

They waited, crouched among the branches, as the white truck came into the sweep of the bay, groaning and rattling in its own dust storm. Closer it came, closer, and then there was a shrill sound of brakes and a great shuddering as the driver pulled up near the package.

He got out to pick it up, but that was the only part of the plan that worked. The truck was too far away from the bank for them to jump. They had to slide down and then haul themselves up onto the truck bed, which was very high off the ground. Nor was there much time. The driver didn't open the package. He took it back to the cab, slammed the door, and put the truck in gear. Hannah and Mikey were on the truck bed, holding the dangling Sky by his wrists. Dust flew up from the wheels, blotting out everything.

Hannah could see only Sky's face, tight with terror. They pulled and pulled. He was too frightened to help them. Gradually he came up over the edge, and Mikey held him tight. Hannah lifted up the edge of the heavy canvas cover. It was laced to the sides but loose enough for them to crawl under.

They huddled together under the canvas. It was hot and dark and so bumpy that their bones shook, but there wasn't much dust under the cover. Hannah breathed deeply, amazed that they had actually done it. She put her arm around Sky, who had stopped crying. She realized from the smell that he'd wet his pants. "Don't worry," she told him. "They'll dry soon."

Under the cover, it was difficult to judge distance. Hannah lifted the canvas a little, expecting the truck to be halfway out of the Sounds, and saw that they were only about five miles from home. This was going to take forever and ever, she thought.

Sky lay against her, sucking his thumb.

"Hey, Sky, do you want a story?"

His thumb came out of his mouth. "Boomy-boomy-nutcake."

"I'll tell you an H.M. adventure."

Mikey groaned. "I'm sick of sheep stories. What about the adventures of a world champion chess player?"

Hannah hesitated. She wasn't good at chess.

Even Sky could beat her. "It's a new H.M. story."

"Oh, all right," said Mikey. "Apricot."

"Apricot," said Sky over his thumb.

"Apricot," said Hannah, crossing her fingers. She picked up her storytelling voice and began: "I told you how the splendorous spirit of Hannibal Megosaurus can go anywhere, didn't I? In the sky, on the water, under the water, through walls—"

"This isn't new!" snorted Mikey.

"Shut up, Mikey. Yes, the spirit of Hannibal Megosaurus goes anywhere she likes and then comes back to the magic place. One day, the spirit of H.M. was away in Nelson, and some people went up the creek. They were really terrible people. They trampled over the magic place. They chopped down trees and pulled out ferns."

"No!" said Sky. "Don't let them do that!"

"It's only a story," Mikey said.

Hannah shifted on the bouncing boards. "They didn't believe in magic. They didn't care about anything. They saw the body of Hannibal Megosaurus on her rock, and they said, 'How utterly gross! It's only the skeleton of an old sheep!' The man said, 'Let's take it away!' and the woman said, 'Why don't we burn it?' 'We'll throw it on the rubbish heap,' said the man. 'Bury it!' said the woman."

Sky sucked in his breath. "I'm scared."

"No, don't be. Just listen. Then the woman said, 'I have a great idea! Why don't we sell this old sheep skeleton to the place where they make bone meal for gardens. We'll get some money for it.' And the man agreed. So they put the body of Hannibal Megosaurus on the back of their truck and took it away. But do you know what happened? There were three birds sitting in a tree, listening and watching. They flew to Nelson and told the spirit of Hannibal Megosaurus what had happened. Was she angry! She came rushing back across the water so fast, everyone thought she was a hurricane going by. She found her body lying on the back of the truck. She stepped into it, and the bones stood up straight. The skeleton began to grow. Bigger, bigger. Skin appeared on it. Ears and eyes and tail. Then the wool grew."

"Like silver clouds," said Sky.

"No. Silver lightning because she was so angry."

"It's more comfortable sitting on your schoolbag," Mikey said.

Hannah ignored him. "Her eyes were huge, like two great red lights, and her teeth were like axes. She was so big she squashed the truck. The people ran away screaming, but they couldn't escape the anger of the great H.M."

"Did they get deaded?" Sky asked.

Hannah hesitated. "No, she didn't kill them. She caught one in each hand and threw them—"

"She doesn't have hands," Sky said.

"One with her front hooves and one with her teeth and threw them into the sea, which was freezing cold and full of jellyfish.

Sky wriggled. "What next?"

"That's all," said Hannah.

"That's not the end," said Sky.

"No," said Hannah. "Endings aren't real. But that's all for now."

"I want something else to happen," said Sky.

"Why don't you two try sitting on your schoolbags?" said Mikey. "It feels just like a cushion."

Hannah found that the forever and ever part of the journey did pass quickly, and soon they came to the paved section of the road. The jolting and noise lessened, the speed picked up, and now they could see behind the truck. What a relief it was to be out of the dust! Hannah held the cover up. They watched the road wind away behind them. They saw paddocks, houses, cows coming out of the milking sheds, and pigs being fed. Cars came up close, then passed in a rush of wind. They waved to the drivers and enjoyed the looks of surprise.

"We'll be in Nelson before lunch," Hannah said, trying to work out what they would do when the truck stopped at the freight yards.

How far was Nelson Transport from the dog food factory?

The question was never to be answered, for as they neared the little township of Havelock, the truck slowed down and stopped. Hannah put her head out. They were outside the police station.

She dropped the cover and hissed. "Lie down!"

They stretched out flat, lying still with fear. "He's going into the police station!" Hannah whispered.

"We're going to be arrested," said Mikey. "I told you we shouldn't have done it."

"It was your idea to go and get Shadrach," Hannah said. She pushed the cover back and cautiously peered over the edge of the truck bed. "He's taking the package in!"

Mikey groaned.

"He hasn't unwrapped it or anything. It's still tied up with the ribbon."

"The police'll unwrap it," said Mikey. "They'll find out it's full of stones."

"So what?"

"So we'll get arrested for two things."

"We haven't done anything wrong," said Hannah. "Anyway, no one can prove it's our package."

"They'll test it for fingerprints," Mikey said.

"Are we going to jail?" Sky asked with real interest.

"Let's get off now," said Mikey.

"Shh!" said Hannah, lying flat again. "The driver's coming back!"

They all lay still under the cover while the driver approached the truck, whistling. The whistle and the sound of his boots went all the way around the truck. Then they heard his door close and the engine start. But he didn't put the truck in gear. There was a new whirring noise. Slowly the back of the truck began to tip.

"Hold on!" Mikey said. There was nothing to hold on to except each other. They began to slide. Up went the truck bed and down they came, slipping out from under the canvas cover and onto the road.

Hannah landed face down with her bag and Sky on top of her. In front of her eyes, there was a pair of cracked, dusty boots. She lifted her head and saw the grinning face of the driver. He had a beard and huge sunglasses that made him look like a beetle.

"Going somewhere?" he asked.

None of them answered. They stood and picked up their bags.

"Nice work!" he said. "Too bad I caught you. You want a free ride? Choose someone else's truck." He laughed. "Go on, off to school with you. Do you good." Still laughing, he went back to his cab. As he drove away through the town, the truck bed fell back into place.

It was a little while before Hannah worked things out. "He thought we'd just gotten on," she said to Mikey. "He thought we lived here."

"It's a wonder he didn't see the dust on us," said Mikey, hitting his sweatshirt and releasing a white film into the air.

"That means he doesn't know we put the package on the road," said Hannah, laughing. "He was just being honest, handing in a package he found."

"We're not going to jail?" asked Sky, looking longingly at the police station.

"Let's move, Boomy-boomy-nutcake," said Hannah. "We're only halfway to Nelson."

"We're not going to walk!" cried Mikey.

"Only as far as the bus stop," Hannah said cheerfully. "There'll be a bus to Nelson soon."

Sky followed them, walking wide-legged in his damp pants but not complaining.

"We've got plenty of money," Hannah said, forgetting they were going to use it to buy back Shadrach. "Let's get some ice cream."

CHAPTER SEVEN

They had over an hour to wait for the Nelson bus. Mikey and Hannah left Sky on the bus station bench, watching the bags, while they went across the road to the store. It was easier buying ice cream without Sky, who could never make up his mind what flavor he wanted.

They looked carefully around the store before they went in just in case there was someone inside who knew them. A lot of people from the Sounds did their shopping in Havelock.

"No deadly spies!" Mikey said cheerfully. "Advance to next position."

Hannah had a fistful of money, and as they stood in line waiting to be served, she looked at the shelves behind the counter. "Bubble gum," she said. "Caramels."

"Vinegar-flavored potato crisps," said Mikey, his mouth watering.

"Licorice all-sorts," said Hannah. "White chocolate. Extra strong peppermints."

"Crisps," said Mikey. "Crunchy brown vinegar crisps."

"What would you like, dear?" the woman behind the counter asked Hannah.

"Three double cones, please," said Hannah. "One strawberry, one goody-gum-drops, and one double chocolate. And I'd like some—"

"Crisps," said Mikey.

"Some vinegar-flavored crisps. Three packets, please."

Hannah had her strawberry ice cream in one hand and her money in the other. She walked ahead of Mikey, who was struggling to keep a cone in each hand and the bags of crisps under his arms. He didn't see what happened. He heard Hannah cry out. Then he saw her ice cream upside down on the floor, looking like a red-faced clown. Instead of trying to pick it up, Hannah simply stood there, her hand over her mouth.

Mikey couldn't do anything to help, but the woman came immediately with paper towels. "Accidents happen all the time. Don't worry, dear. I'll get you another one."

Mikey was about to make a joke of it when Hannah started to cry.

"It doesn't matter," he said, standing there with ice cream running down his hands. Then he saw what was in front of Hannah: a high shelf full of cans. They were stacked two high with large red and white labels: WUFF STUFF.

On each can there was a picture of a dog and the words, "When only the best is good enough, give your pet delicious WUFF STUFF."

"Here you are, dear," said the woman, giving Hannah another ice cream. "Hurry up now. I have a feeling you might be late for school."

Hannah was very quiet after that—no more stories, no more organizing. They sat together on the bench at the bus stop. All of the talk came from Sky, who kept walking up to people and telling them his name was Boomy-boomy-nutcake. Mikey looked out to see if there was anyone they knew. After a while, he relaxed and did things for Hannah like blowing up their crisp bags and bursting them. He went up and down the sidewalk in the front of her doing his squeaky knee trick, walking stiffly like a robot and making creaking noises with his mouth at each step. Usually Hannah laughed at that. He and Sky made faces to look like monsters. But Hannah just sat there, all bundled up inside herself.

Mikey knew how she felt about the cans, but he thought she was overdoing it. He said, "Look, if Mr. Wuff Stuff makes dog food, he's got to sell it to the stores, doesn't he? I mean, they just didn't stick it up on the shelf to freak you out. I bet it's in every store—"

"Shut up!" snapped Hannah.

"Shadrach has Hannibal Megosaurus to look after him," Mikey said.

Even that didn't get through to her. She sat like a statue, only moving when a dog came up to her, trying to be friendly.

"I'm more worried than you are," Mikey said, clutching his heart. "I'm worried about Shadrach. I'm worried about what Joe and Sophie are going to say. I'm worried about the truck driver. The school bus. Missing school. I'm just one big heap of worries. Look!" He made a crazy face.

All she did was fold her arms and turn her head away.

She was all right, though, when the bus stopped. "Three tickets to Nelson," she said to the driver, holding out a handful of crumpled money.

"What, no school today?" he asked.

"We're going to the dentist," Hannah said quickly.

The driver laughed. "Hope that's not too boring for you."

Mikey, who collected jokes, repeated it to himself so that he would remember it. As they sat down, Hannah and Sky in one seat and Mikey in front of them, Hannah spoke at last. "It wasn't much of a lie," she said. "I really feel like we're going to the dentist."

Always before, Mikey had traveled to Nelson by car. Seated high in the coach with a large window to himself, he could see much more scenery. Perhaps that was why he noticed so many dogs and horses on the trip. He hoped that Hannah wasn't looking.

Nearer Nelson, a woman got on and sat beside him. She didn't say anything, but several times she sniffed. He hoped she knew that the smell was coming from Sky and not from him.

They were going past the sea. Mikey counted the wooden houses perched on sand dunes and the boats in front yards. Ahead of them was the city of Nelson—like a jigsaw puzzle waiting to be put together.

"Excuse me," Mikey said to the woman sitting next to him. "Do you know where Harvey Street is?"

"Yes?"

"Harvey Street in Nelson."

"Yes?"

He thought she might be deaf. He shouted. "We want to go to Harvey Street!"

"Please? Yes?"

Then he realized that the woman was a tourist who didn't understand what he was saying.

The woman smiled at him and offered him some candy. He looked at it. He'd always been told never to take candy from strangers, but he supposed this was different. He smiled back. "Thanks."

As they got off the bus, he asked the driver,

"Can you tell us where Harvey Street is?"

"Sure. Out of town that way. First turn left, second right, and keep on going. What do you want Harvey Street for? Nothing much down there. A bit of industrial land, paddocks, an old dog food factory. No dentist."

Hannah said, "First we have to see someone at the dog food factory."

Mikey asked. "Is it easy to find?"

"You'll smell it long before you get there," said the driver. "Just follow your nose, son. Just follow your nose."

CHAPTER EIGHT

Shadrach was still alive.

Hannah could see him while they were still some distance from the factory. He was in a pen, taller than the other horses. As they got closer, they saw that he was still wearing the old rope halter he'd had on two days ago.

"I told you we'd get here in time," Mikey said. He did the craziest of his funny walks, kicking his legs, flapping his arms and yelling, "Yay! Yay! Yay!"

Sky joined in, but Hannah simply stood there, looking at Shadrach and quietly singing inside herself. He was safe. The spirit of Hannibal Megosaurus had indeed protected him. The Wuff Stuff factory appeared to be made up of two concrete-and-iron sheds, one much bigger than the other, with several wooden pens at the back.

Crowded into two of the pens were about twenty horses. Although some of them were restless, most stood like Shadrach: still, heads down, tails flicking at the clouds of flies.

The bus driver was right. There was no escaping the smell of the place. It grew worse as they came closer, a strong odor made up of blood, manure, offal, and the gases of decay. When they crossed the road and stood outside the factory, they saw where the stench was coming from—an open drain the size of a small swimming pool. The drain had a thick, greenish crust on the surface, which was alive with maggots. Above it, a thick swarm of flies filled the air with a droning noise.

The next thing Hannah noticed was that the crowded horses had no water, no food, no kind of shelter. She suspected that Shadrach had been in that dirty pen for at least twenty-four hours. "It's worse than I imagined!"

Sky was chanting, "Ink, pink, pen, and ink. I smell a great big stink!" and was throwing stones at the pond.

"Shadrach!" called Hannah across the rails of the pens. "Shadrach!"

He lifted his head with a quick, eager whinny. Hannah would have climbed through the pens to get to him, but Mikey was already walking around to the front of the building. She followed him.

"I suppose this is the way in," Mikey said. "I wonder where everyone is?"

There was no sign with the name of the factory on it and nothing to tell them where the office was. At the back of the smaller shed they found some open windows and a red painted door, slightly ajar. "The color of blood," Hannah thought.

As they knocked on the door, they peered through the windows and saw a desk, papers, telephone, a calendar with a sports car on it, and a cup half-full of coffee.

Mikey knocked again, and Hannah called out, "Is anyone there?"

No one answered. They pushed the door open.

It did appear to be an office, and behind it, through an open doorway, they saw a warehouse, which was also deserted. To one side there was a loading bay where a large truck half-stacked with cartons and a fork-lift loader were parked. More cartons were piled up against the walls of the warehouse. Each box had a picture of a Wuff Stuff can on every side.

Mikey whistled. "I wonder how many poor old horses are in this shipment."

"Hundreds!" said Sky. "Thousands and millions and zillions!"

"Maybe everyone's gone home for lunch," said Hannah.

"They'd have to go home," Mikey said. "Imagine eating lunch in this stink!"

At the far end of the warehouse, there was an entrance to the next building. As they walked toward it, Hannah felt cheered by the thought that the factory might be deserted. In that case, they could simply take Shadrach out of the pen without having to explain anything. But then Sky said he could hear water running in the next building. They crossed the small yard between the two sheds, and Hannah heard it, too. Somewhere there was a hose splashing over iron and concrete.

Now they were in a room filled with stacks of flattened cardboard boxes tied with string and a bench of Wuff Stuff cans waiting to be packed. Through a door, on a conveyor belt that looked like the tracks of a miniature railway, was a row of cans waiting to move. From the other side of that wall came the splashing sounds of water.

Mikey tugged at the handle of a heavy metal sliding door and made a gap big enough for Hannah to put her head through. She choked on the smell. The air was hot with cooking meat. She saw large steel pressure cookers and the conveyor belt with rows of cans stopped at various stages of packing. A spasm in her stomach went all the way to her throat, and she thought she might be sick.

A man in a plastic apron was washing the walls and floor with a high-pressure hose that made so much noise that Hannah's call went unheard.

She pushed against the sliding door until she was able to get into the room. She tried not to look to the left, where carcasses hung on hooks from high railings and knives lay on benches next to the vats. Her skin felt hot and cold. Her head floated in giddiness. She couldn't throw up here! With fingers crossed she muttered, "Apricot, apricot, apricot!"

Mikey and Sky came through the door behind her and were staring around the room. Hannah went nearer the man, calling, "Excuse me!"

She said it several times, but the water drowned out her voice completely and he didn't turn toward her. She wondered how she could get his attention. She saw that the hose was connected to a faucet on the wall. She went across to turn it off.

The faucet was not like any of those at home. It was round like a wheel and mounted sideways against the wall. In her confusion, Hannah turned it the wrong way.

The hose leaped out of the man's hands and sprang up like an angry snake. All by itself, it lashed back and forth, shooting water over everyone and everything. The man yelled and tried to grab it. He was thrust back by the force of the water. In seconds they were all soaked. When the spray hit them, it knocked them over and sent them skidding across the floor, breathless with the shock of it. Just as they got to their feet, it hit them again, and down they went.

Then it stopped. The man had turned off the faucet.

Now there was another fury. The man yelled at them and waved his arms.

Hannah struggled to her feet, weighed down by the wet schoolbag over her shoulders. Mikey was helping Sky, who had been swept under a bench and was crying loudly.

"I'm sorry! I'm sorry!" Hannah kept saying.

He didn't stop shouting long enough to listen to her. "You know what happens to kids who snoop around here?" He pointed to the pressure cookers. "They disappear!"

Sky screamed, his arms tight around Mikey.

"He doesn't mean it," Hannah said, "It isn't true."

"It's true, all right." The man was very red in the face and very wet. "You get out of here, and don't come back."

"I really am sorry," Hannah said. "I was trying to turn it off. I wanted to talk to you."

"Out! Out! Out!"

"We were looking for the manager."

"I am the manager. If you're not out of here in ten seconds—"

Sky was already running out the door, with Mikey following him.

Hannah was left to talk to the furious man. "Please listen! It's important. There's been a terrible mistake!"

He stopped yelling and asked, "What kind of mistake?"

"Two mistakes!" said Hannah. "I honestly didn't mean to get you wet. Your faucet is different—"

"What's the other mistake?"

The fact that he'd stopped shouting made Hannah more confident. She said, "It's our horse, Shadrach, the big draft horse who came in yesterday. He's not supposed to be here."

The man was wiping water off his clothes with the flat of his hand. "Out!" he said.

"No, listen! You can't kill him. They—they sent the wrong horse. We have to take him back."

"No mistake, kid. I paid cash on delivery for that animal. He's mine."

"We'll buy him back." Hannah felt in her pocket and brought out a sopping handful of money. "Here's a deposit. I'll mail the rest." She saw him getting angry again and said quickly, "Joe and Sophie—that's my father and mother—they said we couldn't go home without him."

"Did they now?" snorted the man. "Right!"

He put his heavy hand on Hannah's shoulder and steered her toward the sliding door. "We'll find out, shall we?"

In the packing room, above the bench where the cans of dog food were waiting to be put into cartons, there was a phone. Hannah felt a deep heaviness. She needed Mikey and Sky. Where were they?

The man picked up the phone. "Out in the Marlborough Sounds, isn't it? What's the number?"

Hannah stared at him, mouth open.

"Come on. We'll talk to your mom and dad and see what they have to say." The man grinned at her.

"I—I—" Hannah didn't know what to say.

But the man wasn't listening to her. He turned his head and said, "What's that?"

She listened. Outside the building there was a restless whinnying.

"They're fooling around with the horses!" the man said, dropping the phone without bothering to hang it up. He ran back through the sliding door.

Fearing for Mikey and Sky, Hannah ran after him. She went past the vats, past the carcasses hanging from the rails. She hesitated. The area in front of her would have to be the place where the killing was done. She ran on. At the end was an open doorway, and the man was standing there, relaxed now, leaning against the door frame, his thumbs hooked in the pockets of his jeans.

Hannah went on until she could see beyond him. In front of the doorway and to the left was the open drain they'd looked at earlier. On the right, the horses in the two pens were nervously pawing the ground and snorting. Shadrach was not among them. He was on the other side of the railing, being led away by Mikey. Sky was closing the gate after him.

Neither Mikey nor Sky knew the man was watching them. Nor did the man speak. He stood back in the shadow of the doorway, smiling to himself. He let Mikey and Sky take Shadrach around the pens. Then, when they were close to the doorway, he stepped out and said, "I'll take that."

Mikey dropped Shadrach's rope. He and Sky walked slowly backward.

The man grinned at them as he picked up the rope. "Killing starts this afternoon," he said. "Thanks for bringing this one to me. He can be first."

"No!" shrieked Sky. "No, no, no, no!"

"You can't kill him!" howled Hannah.

"Can't I? Just you stay around and watch!" The man moved back toward the door that led to the killing area, and Shadrach meekly followed him.

Hannah took a deep breath. She bellowed, "Bow down, Shadrach!"

The man hesitated, and Shadrach tossed his head.

"Bow down!" Hannah yelled.

Sky and Mikey took up the cry. "Bow down, Shadrach! Bow down, Shadrach!"

The old horse snorted, rocked for a moment, and then reared up on his hind legs. His ears were flat, his lips curled back, and his great hairy hooves flailed at the air close to the manager's head. The man got frightened and put up his hands to protect himself. At the same time, he ducked back. His foot slipped at the edge of the drain. In the next instant there was a splash. The Wuff Stuff manager went down through the foul crust, sending up flies and a terrible stench.

Shadrach came down again on four legs as the Wuff Stuff man struggled to his feet in the pond.

Hannah giggled from sheer nervousness. The factory manager was covered with a thick, green and brown slime. If anyone needed a pressure hose, he did. He looked like something from a horror movie, and the smell was awful. Each time he tried to climb out of the drain, he slipped back again. Hannah didn't know what to do. She couldn't give him her hand.

"Hurry up, Hannah!" Mikey called. He was

leading Shadrach across the road. And Sky—
where was Sky? Then Hannah realized that all
the other horses were coming out of the pens.
Sky had opened their gates and was chasing
them out onto the road.

The Wuff Stuff man realized what was happening. With a cry, he leaped at the bank, his
fingers scrabbling at the concrete. Slowly, he
pulled himself out of the drain. He stood up,
roaring like something wounded, and Hannah
was afraid he'd come after her. But by now the
other horses were far down the road. The man
went after them, running, dripping, and shouting noises too indistinct for words.

Hannah was surprised that the mob of horses
had moved so quickly. Shadrach, on the other
hand, hobbled very slowly across the road. Perhaps bowing down had twisted the ligament
again.

"Sky, you're a genius," Hannah said.

"That's not my name," he said, looking
pleased with himself.

"I'm glad we brought you with us, Boomy-
boomy-nutcake. You've saved us! I hereby grant
you the medal of absolute genius." She picked
up a bottle cap from the road and placed it in
his hand.

"I deserve the medal of wetness," said Mikey.
"I'm soaked to my skin. Under my skin! I might
just dissolve away."

"We'll dry out," said Hannah, full of optimism although she was shivering.

Shadrach was obviously hungry, for he kept stopping to eat grass through fences. The mob of horses had now disappeared, and so had the man. But Hannah expected him back at any time. "Come on, Shadrach!"

"It's no use trying to hurry him," Mikey said. "He can't. That's why the guy went after the rest. He knew we couldn't get far."

Mikey was right. Hannah's moment of rejoicing left her.

"He'll cook us!" Sky cried. "He'll make us into dog food."

"No, he won't," said Hannah. "But he'll kill Shadrach."

"And get us into a lot of trouble," said Mikey.

"We'd better hide!" Sky said.

It was a sensible suggestion, but where? Hannah looked around. There were no houses in this area, only open grassland, small trees that wouldn't hide a cat, some empty oil drums in a fenced yard with locked gates, a school, and a gas station. She pulled on Shadrach's halter. "This is no time to be thinking of your stomach!"

Sky picked a bunch of grass and held it in front of the horse's nose. Shadrach moved then, very slowly, while Sky walked with the grass, chanting, "Ink, pink, pen, and ink. I'm not scared of Mr. Stink!"

Mikey said to Hannah, "When Mr. Stink comes back, you know what we'll have to do, don't you?"

"What?"

"Leave Shadrach here and run for it."

"No!" cried Hannah, a sudden pain inside her. "We're not leaving him!" She crossed her fingers. "We'll find a place to hide."

"But there isn't a place," Mikey insisted.

"Think hard," said Hannah. "Think very hard, and we'll find one."

CHAPTER NINE

Getting him up the steps was the hardest part. Hannah bribed while Mikey threatened, and Sky, holding both doors open, kept yelling at them to hurry.

Hannah waved a bunch of grass under Shadrach's nose, saying, "You don't realize that this is a matter of life or death. *Your* life, Shadrach!"

At the other end, Mikey pushed and growled, "Move, you big dog's dinner!"

After much balking and snorting, Shadrach suddenly changed his mind and lurched up the steps, straight through the entrance, and into the hallway of the school. Sky and Mikey quickly closed the doors.

It was a small school, with only four class-rooms off the main hall. They had no trouble coaxing Shadrach into the nearest classroom, because the sweet smell of apples from school lunches hung in the air. They moved a couple of old, wooden desks aside to give the huge horse a place to stand. The clomp, clomp of his hooves on the floor made Hannah and Mikey nervous.

"You stay here, Mikey, while I check to make sure everyone has gone home for the day," Hannah whispered.

"While you're at it, see if you can find a bucket in the janitor's closet, and bring Shadrach some water," Mikey hissed. "He's terribly thirsty."

"Why are you whispering?" asked Sky. "Don't you think anyone can hear the clompity-clomp? If there's anyone here."

"Shhhhhhh," cautioned Hannah, although she knew Sky was right, and she crept out into the hall.

"Mikey, look at these picture books. Read me this story about a horse. Please? Please?" begged Sky.

"Not now," said Mikey, taking his schoolbag off his shoulders. Like the rest of him, his lunch bag had been soaked by the runaway hose, but fortunately the lunch inside was covered with plastic. He began to unwrap it but then saw that it was squashed—six sandwiches turned into one soggy mass of bread, lettuce, and peanut butter. He remembered that he'd used his bag as a cushion in the freight truck, and he felt worse because he could only blame himself. He was hungry, but he'd have to be starving to death to eat that mess.

Soon Hannah returned with a plastic bucket of water. "All clear," she sighed as she set the bucket in front of Shadrach, who drank quickly and noisily. "Poor thirsty horse," said Hannah, kissing him on the nose. "I'll get you some more."

"Do you think you should?" Mikey asked. He was aware that the marks they were making with their wet clothes and shoes would be nothing compared with a puddle from Shadrach, and this was a school, not a barn.

"I bet he's had nothing to drink for two days," said Hannah.

"We could be in here for ages," Mikey reminded her, "at least until it's dark and Mr. Stink has gone home. We can't go out while he's looking for us."

"One of us can," said Hannah. "They'll have a phone at the gas station. One of us can sneak out and call Sophie and Joe."

Mikey thought about that. "What if they say we have to take Shadrach back to the factory?"

"We won't do it," Hannah said crisply.

Mikey winced. "More problems!"

"They started all this," Hannah said. "They're the ones in the wrong. I'm going to get him another bucket of water."

Mikey sat down at a desk. "Well, here we are in school today after all." He tried to joke, but his voice caught. Hannah was already out the door to get more water. "We're in big trouble," he moaned. "Big, big trouble."

"Please, Mikey, read to me." Sky plopped a pile of books in Mikey's lap.

"Maybe later," said Mikey as Hannah crept in the door with another bucket of water.

Shadrach drank the second bucket of water as eagerly as the first. Mikey jumped up and blocked Hannah's move to fill the bucket a third time. In the end, she put the bucket down, and they all examined their lunches to see if there was anything worth eating. Hannah's sandwiches were as squashed as Mikey's, but Sky's were fine because they'd been packed in his plastic lunch box. They had one peanut butter and lettuce sandwich each and shared an apple bite by bite.

Hannah looked at Mikey. "Who's going to phone home?"

"You!" said Mikey quickly.

"We'll toss," said Hannah, taking a coin from her pocket.

"You can tell them better," Mikey pleaded. "You know what to say."

"Heads or tails?"

"It was your idea."

"And it was you who gave the idea to me. Heads or tails?"

"Heads."

The coin came up heads as he knew it would. He made a face and stood up. "Where's the money?"

"You don't need money. Make it a collect call."

Mikey opened the school door slowly, just in case the Wuff Stuff man was outside. He wasn't. The road was clear. He walked to the corner of the building, flattening himself against the wall like someone from a cops-and-robbers movie. He could see the dog food factory in the distance but couldn't smell it. There were no horses either.

Feeling more confident, he ran down the road to the gas station.

The area by the gas pumps was fully taken up by a green truck and an old camping trailer the same color. At first Mikey thought the truck was towing a horse trailer, but that was only because he had horses and trailers on his mind. It was a camping trailer all right, with small windows shuttered with venetian blinds and a propane tank on the front. It must belong to the elderly man and woman who were in the gas station buying a map, Mikey thought.

He looked around for a public phone. There wasn't one. He would have to wait and ask the attendant if he could use his.

The attendant was in no hurry. He opened the map in front of the couple and showed them places of scenic interest on the South Island. "When you get down the West Coast, you must visit the pancake rocks at Punakaiki."

"I remember those from years back!" the man exclaimed. "But Marge here has never been to the South Island before. My cousin in Nelson has loaned us his rig for a few weeks."

Mikey fidgeted, glancing every now and then at the road.

"Here's the Franz Joseph Glacier," said the attendant, drawing another circle on the map. "If you don't want to walk, they have helicopter rides... Hey! Listen to this!" He suddenly reached across the counter and turned up the radio.

The newswoman's voice filled the gas station. "...an unusual sight in the streets of Nelson today as a dozen or more horses joined pre-Christmas shoppers in several stores. A publicity stunt? Apparently not. According to Craig Benny of Harvey Road, the horses were released from his pet food factory this afternoon..."

"They were here!" cried the attendant. "I saw them go past!"

Mikey stood absolutely still.

"It was a stampede!" the attendant laughed.

"...So if you should find an elderly nag in your garden or lurking behind the shelves of your local supermarket, please contact Craig Benny, the manager..."

The attendant turned down the volume. "Vandals," he said. "Some kids opened the gates."

Mikey wondered if he should run, but while he had in his head a picture of himself racing away with the attendant close behind, his feet stayed on the black rubber mat of the gas station floor.

"Poor old horses," said the man.

"I'm so glad they got away," the woman said.

"Where are you heading tonight?" the attendant asked, turning back to the map.

The woman replied, "We want to go to Havelock to see where Lord Ernest Rutherford lived. You know? The man who discovered how to split the atom? We thought we'd stay there tonight. Does Havelock have a campground?"

"Oh sure! Right down by the shore. There won't be many campers this time of year. Easy journey—about an hour and a half from here."

"Thank you," said the woman. "You are very kind."

"One more thing," the man said. "Is there a place around here where we can get something to eat?"

"Not on Harvey Street, but if you go down half a block and turn right, you'll find a seafood place.

Best fish and chips in Nelson. Tell them Ewan from the gas station sent you."

"Can we leave the camping rig here?" the man asked.

"Sure! Park it around by the side, and it'll be fine."

As the man and woman left, Mikey stepped forward. "Excuse me," he said with perfect politeness. "I don't want to bother you, but please, may I use your phone?"

"No," said the attendant.

Mikey didn't know what to say. He watched the attendant tidying up a rack of road maps. "It's for a collect call," he said in a weak voice.

"Plenty of phone booths in town," said the attendant. "I keep this phone for me and my customers." He looked hard at Mikey. "You been swimming with your clothes on?"

Mikey turned and went out quickly, his heart beating like a drum. It would be his kind of luck if the attendant was a friend of the Wuff Stuff man.

Between the gas station and the school, he stopped to look at the elderly couple who were having some difficulty backing the truck and trailer into a parking space at the side of the gas station. After several attempts, they left the trailer at an awkward angle, got out, and walked down the street arm in arm.

When they were well out of sight, Mikey walked over to the trailer, measuring it with his eye. The door had an ordinary latch with no space for a key, but was it wide enough?

He ran back to the school, calling softly as he went in, "It's all right. Only me."

Hannah pounced on him. "What did they say?"

"I didn't call them. I couldn't. The guy wouldn't let me use the phone."

"You were away for a long time!" said Sky.

"I couldn't help it. I had to wait to ask him." He grabbed Hannah's arm. "I want to show you something."

"What?"

Mikey took her to the front door. "See that green truck and trailer over there? It belongs to two old people who like horses. Look at the door; it isn't locked. Do you think we could get him in?"

Hannah stared. "I—I don't know."

"Because if we can," said Mikey, "I think we have a ride as far as Havelock."

CHAPTER TEN

After lunch, Sophie and Joe decided to clean out the chicken house. Joe needed the old straw for his pumpkin patch in the orchard, and Sophie thought that if they worked together they might get both jobs completed before the children came home from school. The rest of the day could then be spent in some family activity.

"Weather's good," she said. "We could have a bonfire on the beach. Roast potatoes. Ghost stories. Singing with guitars. All that stuff."

"You have to let them grieve," said Joe, forking out straw from under the perches. "You can't hurry it or cover it over with a party."

"I know, I know," said Sophie. "I'm feeling my own grief for Hannah. She's in such pain, Joe. Maybe we'll just have a bonfire and a quiet family talk, eh?"

"Okay," said Joe. "Let's get it over with."

"You mean tell them he's dead?"

"Better sooner than later."

"How? Heart attack? Died in his sleep?" Sophie piled the straw into the wheelbarrow.

"Sleep," said Joe. "And we'd better get it right, because they're going to ask lots of questions."

"Sky will want to know about a funeral. He's been really big on funerals since Grandpa died."

"We'll say he was cremated."

"Can you cremate a horse?"

"I don't see why not." Joe stood up, leaning on the fork. "It would have been simpler to have told them the truth in the first place."

"What?" said Sophie. "Joe, in the face of an impossibly harsh fact, we chose gentle fiction. They're good, loving kids. They deserve a good, loving story." She picked up the handles of the barrow. "Where do you want this dumped?"

They sprayed the chicken house for mites, put in fresh straw, and then went down to the orchard to layer the straw with compost on the pumpkin patch and water it for planting. They had almost finished when Maree Gerritsen's yellow truck came into sight. She stopped on the road near the orchard fence and called out, "More giant pumpkins?"

"Hello, Maree!" Sophie called back. "You're not teaching today?"

"This morning only." Maree got out of the truck with a large plastic bottle and leaned over the fence. "I brought some homemade root beer down for the children. It's been bounced around a bit. Tell them to be careful taking the top off."

"Wow! Root beer!" Joe walked over to the fence. "Thanks, Maree. They'll love it. We'll put it in the fridge until they come home from school."

Maree looked puzzled. "I thought they were home."

"Not yet."

"They're not at school."

Sophie came over to join them. "Our children? Hannah and Mikey and Sky?"

"They haven't been at school all day," said Maree.

"They went on the bus this morning." Sophie's voice was tense.

"No. I waited and honked."

"But I saw them walking down the drive. Hannah was wearing her pink sweatshirt. Sky had his new reading book."

"You mean you haven't seen them all day?" Joe asked.

Maree shook her head. "Hans said that Mikey and Hannah were pretty upset yesterday. He just thought you'd kept them home. I should have checked."

"Upset?" said Sophie.

"Hans read a note that Mikey wrote to Hannah in class. It was about Shadrach and the pet food factory."

"But they didn't know about that!" Sophie said.

Maree smiled and shook her head. "Everyone at school knows."

Sophie and Joe looked at each other, amazed at their stupidity. They should have realized. In a place like this? Of course they should have known.

"They've run away," said Sophie. "That's what they've done."

"Gone to Nelson," Joe said.

"But how would they get out of the Sounds?" Sophie asked. "No one's going to give a ride to three children without asking questions." She glanced at Joe. "No one who could be trusted."

"Don't worry," said Maree. "They won't be out of the Sounds. Probably just a ways down the road. Do you want me to go and look for them?"

"Thanks, Maree," said Joe, "but we have to go."

"They'd better be all right!" said Sophie in sudden anger. "They'd better be okay, that's all."

Joe knew she was close to tears. He put his arms around her. "Of course they're okay. You put some gas in the car. I'm going back to the house to phone the Wuff Stuff factory."

While Joe was away, Maree helped Sophie fill the car from the farm's gas tank. She listened while Sophie told her about the Home for Aged Equestrian Friends.

"We couldn't tell them!" Sophie said. "Not Hannah. You know what the girl's like. She'd never get over it."

"She knows now," Maree said.

"The best thing that can happen is that, as you say, they're down the road a ways. We pick them up and bring them home. You know what the worst thing is? Somehow they get to Nelson and go to that dog food place. He was being killed today. Right now he's being—well, whatever they do to them."

"There's no way they could have gotten to Nelson. No one would have given them a ride," Maree insisted.

Joe came running back. As he came close, Sophie saw that he was smiling, and her fear disappeared.

"They're in Nelson," Joe said. "They're all right."

"How did they get there?" Sophie asked.

"Who gave them a lift?" asked Maree.

"I haven't a clue!" Joe laughed, then put his hands over his head in a gesture of despair. "What do you want first? Comedy? Tragedy? The manager says he's going to sue us."

"They took Shadrach!" Sophie cried.

"Yes. They took Shadrach. According to Mr. Craig Benny, they also flooded his factory. They released eighteen valuable horses and chased them through the town. And—get this—they tried to drown Benny in a cesspool."

"No!" said Sophie. "They wouldn't do those things!"

"He says he's been trying to call us all afternoon. He wants three thousand dollars damages. I asked him if he's called the police. For some obscure reason he hasn't. Nor did he like the idea."

"They tried to drown him?" Sophie asked.

"They were there about two hours ago. He hasn't seen them since. They won't be hard to find. Shadrach's not your average-sized pet. Hop in, Sophie."

"Joe, I just know they wouldn't do things like that!"

"Honey, of course they wouldn't. Craig Benny is the least of our worries. Those kids'll be tired and hungry. They've got a horse that's ready to collapse on top of them. And it's three hours to Nelson. Let's go."

"My parents live near Nelson," said Maree. "I'll ask them to do a little searching around."

"Thanks, Maree. We'll keep in touch by phone in case you hear anything."

Maree smiled. "I'll put the root beer in your fridge."

Joe chose to drive. He went faster than usual, skidding on the gravel, swinging around corners, leaving a long plume of dust behind them. On the paved surface of the main road, he increased his speed. They rocketed through Havelock, well above the speed limit, overtaking every vehicle in front of them.

Sophie asked him to slow down.

"They're our kids," said Joe. "It's an emergency."

"It'll be an emergency if we have an accident," Sophie said. "Three kids without parents."

And they almost did have an accident. On the winding hill road near Nelson, Joe had to swerve violently to miss a green truck pulling a large camping trailer.

Chapter Eleven

Margery and David Schumaker had always lived in Auckland, and they were looking forward to a two-week vacation on the South Island. David had been south briefly when he was a young man, but for Margery this was a first trip, and she had been planning it for months.

David was no longer sure they could do all of their intended sightseeing. The borrowed trailer was not what he had expected, and he thought that maybe they should just stick to the main highways.

That morning they had flown from Auckland to Wellington and then across Cook Straight to Nelson. David's cousin had met them at the airport with the truck and trailer, all ready to go. David had tried to appear grateful, but secretly he had been dismayed. The truck had gears, whereas he was used to an automatic transmission, and the trailer was a heavy, homemade thing with a single axle. It wobbled dangerously at highway speed.

He had thought the trailer was difficult to tow from the airport parking lot, but now, on the road from Nelson to Havelock, it seemed much worse—very sluggish, too wide for the narrow road over the hills. On some of the steeper slopes, he was down to second gear and still the truck was crawling. Cars were jammed up behind him. He couldn't always find a place to pull over and let them pass. They traveled with a chorus of honking.

Then a car came toward them very fast, nearly finishing their vacation before it had started. Fortunately, the driver was able to swerve away at the last second. They were left feeling weak with shock. It was just as well, David said to Margery, that they were only going as far as Havelock that day. He wasn't feeling up to driving farther.

They found the campground easily, thanks to the directions given to them by the man at the Nelson gas station. They went together to the office to register and select a campsite.

As had been predicted, the campground was almost empty, and they were able to choose a site with a view of the sea. David would set up the trailer while Margery went inside to find the cord for the power outlet.

David heard her cry out.

He left what he was doing and ran around to the door.

Margery was inside pointing to the floor and saying, "What's that?"

David knew from the smell what it was, even before he saw it. In the middle of the trailer floor was a large pile of horse manure.

Chapter Twelve

Havelock was less than fifty miles from home, but it could have been on the other side of the world as far as Hannah was concerned. They were all cold and hungry, and they had a horse that refused to take another step. Shadrach had walked from the campground along the shore to the boat marina. Now he wouldn't budge.

They knew it was late afternoon. Children were playing in the boatyard. The light hung low over the sea, patching it with fire and dark shade. A cool sea breeze stirred every now and then to make them shiver in their clothes, which were still damp. They bought some apple juice and drank it to wash down the squashed sandwiches. Mikey was in a grumpy mood and kept nagging about the floor of the trailer.

"Oh, be quiet, Mikey! Do you realize that people pay money for that stuff? They do! It's good for growing roses."

"There were no roses growing in the trailer," Mikey said.

"Didn't smell like roses," Sky grinned.

Hannah felt that they were ganging up on her. "It wasn't my suggestion to hitch a ride in a trailer."

"I suggested it because they were nice people," said Mikey. "They liked horses. I thought they'd probably find out we were there, but they'd let us ride anyway."

"Okay, so they got a souvenir. Don't keep talking about it."

"I'm not. I just said we should have cleaned it up."

"Yah-yah-yah-yah!" shouted Sky, his hands over his ears.

Hannah looked around to see if anyone was watching. The marina was quiet. Children played among the old boats. Two men talked near the charter yacht office. Between the jetty and the ramp, Wally Yates's old mussel barge rose and fell gently on a lazy tide.

Hannah went over to Shadrach and leaned her head against his chest, listening to his racing heart. His head was down, his body hunched up. He was more tired than any of them.

"Time for you to phone home," Hannah said, looking at Mikey.

"I went last time."

"You didn't make a phone call, though."

"No, but I got you a ride, didn't I?"

"You have to phone! You won the toss!" Hannah was shouting again.

"I'm not going to." Mikey folded his arms.

"I'll do it," Sky offered.

"Thanks Sky—Boomy-boomy-nutcake," said Hannah. "But you can stay here with Shadrach. Mikey and I will both go and call home."

"I'm not going!" said Mikey, and he was crying.

Hannah stamped with frustration. "I'm sick of this! I'm sick of everybody! I wish I could get on a boat with Shadrach and go home!"

Mikey didn't say anything.

"I'll call Sophie and Joe!" said Hannah. "I'm not scared like some people!" She walked away, but farther along the marina she turned, hoping that Mikey was following her. He was still with Sky, staring out to sea. She stood for a moment looking beyond them to the mussel barge near the ramp. Maybe it wasn't such a bad idea to go home by boat. She had planned to ask Sophie and Joe to find them a horse trailer, but what about a barge instead? Something like Wally Yates's mussel barge? Shadrach would be all right on that in a calm sea.

On the way up to the main road, she stopped at the marine supply store and asked the woman, "Do you know where Mr. Yates is?"

"Gone," the woman said.

"His barge is down at the wharf."

"Barge, yes. Wally, no. He's gone to Nelson and won't be back until tomorrow morning."

"Oh." Hannah felt flat. "Okay. Thanks."

She walked along the street, counting footsteps to the phone booth. Seven was her lucky number, and by crowding in one extra step, she got seventy-seven. When she was inside the phone booth, she looked out and saw a pet sheep with a collar and chain, grazing in front of a house. That was more good luck. The spirit of Hannibal Megosaurus was trying to tell her something. She put in the coin and dialed the number. Too bad if Sophie and Joe were mad at her. It was all their fault, anyway.

The phone rang and rang. She could imagine it there on the end of the counter, filling the kitchen with noise. Sophie and Joe should be in the house by now. But there was no answer.

Hannah hung up and got her money back. They'd be out searching, that's where they'd be. They probably knew it all by now—the radio broadcast, the Wuff Stuff man, maybe even the freight truck and the school and the trailer. They could be with the police, planning a huge search with helicopters and all that stuff.

What should she do next?

There was always Mr. Gerritsen. She thought of school yesterday and how kind he'd been when he'd read the note Mikey gave her.

She'd call him. Surely he would know someone in Havelock with a horse trailer.

This time the answer was immediate. It was Mrs. Gerritsen.

"Can I please speak to Mr. Gerritsen?" Hannah asked.

"Is that you, Hannah?" Mrs. Gerritsen spoke as though she had expected a call.

"Yes."

"Where are you?"

"Havelock."

"Are your brothers with you?"

"Yes. Sort of. Can I talk to Mr. Gerritsen?"

She heard their voices in exchange, and then her teacher was on the phone. "Are you all right, Hannah?" he asked in a gentle voice.

"Yes. We're in Havelock. There's Mikey and Sky and me, and we've got Shadrach back. He was in a terrible place. They were going to kill him. Mr. Gerritsen, we need a horse trailer—"

"And Mikey and Sky—are they all right, too?"

"Yes."

"Where exactly in Havelock are you?"

"The phone booth. The others are down by the marina, but Shadrach can't walk anymore. We have to find a trailer. I called Sophie and Joe, but they're not at home."

"I know where they are, Hannah, and I can get a message to them to let them know you're okay. Don't worry about anything, Hannah.

It's all going to be fine. Now listen, Hannah. I want you to hang up the phone and go back to the marina with the others. Wait there. I'll be calling a friend in Havelock who'll come and get you and look after you until your parents arrive."

"What about Shadrach?"

"Shadrach will be looked after. They'll find a paddock for him. Don't worry. The main thing is that you and Mikey and Sky are in a safe place until your mom and dad take you home."

"But we can't go home without Shadrach," Hannah said.

There was a short silence; then Mr. Gerritsen answered, "He'll be looked after in Havelock."

"No!" said Hannah. "He has to go home with us. That's why we need a horse trailer."

"Hannah, you go back to the others. Don't move from the boat marina. These people are very nice. They'll know your names. Remember, Hannah, you won't have to worry about anything."

Hannah put down the phone and stood in the phone booth, her heart beating fast. She knew what was going to happen. Sophie and Joe would take them home, and Shadrach would be sent back to Nelson.

She slammed out of the phone booth and ran as fast as she could back to the marina.

Mikey and Sky came to meet her. "What's happening?" Mikey asked.

She went right past them and down to the jetty. She looked down at the mussel barge. Yes, the key had been left in it.

"What are you doing?" Mikey called.

Out of breath, she said. "They're coming for us. Help me! Shadrach! Got to get him on the barge."

"That's Mr. Yates's boat!" cried Mikey.

"We're borrowing it."

"No!" Mikey stepped backward, his eyes wide. "No, Hannah! You can't."

"I can, and I'm going to. He won't be back till tomorrow. We'll return it. He won't mind. Mikey, they're going to send Shadrach back to the dog food factory!"

"Please, Hannah, don't take it! You can't drive it. Please!"

"I can so drive it. It's no different from our boat. Come on! Don't stand there growing moss."

It was Sky who helped Hannah pull out the broad gangplank and set it in the water in the middle of the boat-launching ramp. Hannah told them about the phone call. Mikey didn't say anything. He didn't try to help.

Sky got behind Shadrach, Hannah in front. They got him one step at a time down to the water's edge and then onto the gangplank. Every step, he stopped for a while. He was breathing fast with a loud, snoring noise.

Finally, he was on the barge.

Hannah and Sky pulled up the gangplank while Mikey watched from the shore. "It's stealing!" he yelled.

"It isn't!"

"You'll go to jail!"

"We've done so much already we will probably go to jail anyway."

Then he said, "Hannah, I think that's the car!"

"Where?" Hannah looked and saw an old red car coming down to the marina. "Moorings!" she yelled. "Mikey, you do the bow line. Sky, untie the stern."

Mikey made up his mind. He ran along the jetty to the front of the barge. Sky stood on the barge near the stern, his arms folded.

"Sky, hurry! Cast off the stern line!" Hannah turned the key, and the engine started with a satisfying roar.

The car was approaching faster now, coming straight for the wharf. There were two people in it.

"Sky!" Hannah shrieked. "The stern line!"

He shook his head, his eyes screwed shut.

"Boomy-boomy-nutcake!" cried Hannah.

Then he was running, but Mikey was already there. The line was off the post, and Mikey leaped down onto the barge.

At the edge of the jetty, the car had stopped. A man and a woman got out, calling their names.

"Hannah! Mikey! Sky! Stop!"

"I'm not Sky!" Sky yelled back.

Hannah pushed the throttle lever forward and felt the boat gears engage. The man and woman ran onto the jetty.

"Stop! Please!"

The barge chugged into the middle of the marina. Hannah thought that the man and woman would surely get into another boat and come after them. But they didn't do that. They stood on the jetty for a while and then went back to their car.

"Hold on to Shadrach just in case he gets scared," said Hannah, steering the boat into the channel. But Shadrach looked too tired to be scared of anything.

The tide was getting low, and the channel was well-defined, a snake of brown water winding through mud flats. Hannah watched the marker beacons. She had been to Havelock many times in the boat with Joe and Sophie, and she knew how easy it was to run aground if you got on the wrong side of the markers. This boat was heavier in the rudder than their own mussel boat, and there was no box for her to stand on. She knelt on the seat, leaning forward on the wheel. The boat chugged evenly over water so calm there was barely a swell. Shadrach had gone back to his drooping position but was bracing himself against movement.

Hannah could see the muscles flex under his skin. Mikey and Sky came back to be with her in the cockpit. Mikey was still anxious, Sky triumphant.

"I'm going to tell everyone at school we brung Shadrach home by ourselves," he said.

Hannah relaxed a little.

Mikey kept saying, "You've really done it this time. Boy, you've really done it."

The list of the day's events had grown so long that Hannah was beyond caring. She still carried within her a strong sense of betrayal. Any blame for the things that had happened she placed squarely with Sophie and Joe.

She had never driven a boat as big as the mussel barge, and the thrill of getting it out of the Havelock channel made her sing inside herself again. She felt so alive that even her toes and fingers were alert, fizzy with electricity. Before dark they'd be safely home, Shadrach back in his paddock beside the house.

The tide was turning. Fish were feeding, and so were the sea birds. Gulls and terns circled, gannets dropped like stones, shearwaters and shags bobbed up and down in the busy water. There were no other boats around. Trees and ferns colored the water dark green, almost black in the shadows. The hills, lit by the last of the sunlight, folded against themselves, one upon another, in shades of lavender and blue.

"When we get home," said Mikey, "I'm going to make a huge plate full of pancakes. We'll have them with brown sugar and butter and lemon juice, and I'll never eat squashed sandwiches again."

The peaceful chugging of the boat's engine echoed around the bush-enclosed bays. In the distance, the lights on the mussel farms were blinking. Day was quickly disappearing.

Hannah kept the boat close to the shore because none of them had life jackets. That was something Sophie had taught them. But she worried about the fast approaching darkness and realized they wouldn't get home before night. She didn't know where the navigation lights were on the vessel. She asked Mikey to look for them.

"I'm not touching anything," he said.

"Just look for the switches!"

"You stole the boat. You look!"

"I notice you didn't stay behind in Havelock," Hannah fired back.

"Stop fighting!" said Sky.

"I had no choice," said Mikey. "I had to come with you. But I'm not going to be your accomplice."

"I only borrowed the barge!"

"You don't borrow things without permission!"

"Stop! Stop!" cried Sky.

And at that moment, they all stopped. A soft bump had Shadrach scrambling to stay on his hooves. The boat came to a halt, the propellor whining and muddy water spraying up behind them.

"Rats!" cried Hannah. She pushed the lever down to reverse. The engine raced, and water boiled brown. But the boat didn't move.

"We've run aground," Sky said needlessly.

Hannah tried again and again, but each effort seemed to settle the boat more firmly into the mud by the shore. Mikey reached over the side with a boat hook and measured the water. "It's less than three feet deep."

Hannah was in a predicament. The tide was coming in and would lift them clear in an hour or so. But she was almost certain that by now the people in Havelock would have found a boat and would be coming after them.

"We can easily wade ashore," Mikey said.

"Why can't we stay on the boat?" said Sky. "Tide's coming in."

Hannah switched off the engine. At once the wide open silence of early evening was upon them. Within that hush there were tiny water noises and the late calls of bellbirds. Hannah put the anchor over the side. The noise of the rattling chain was like gunfire. "We'll go ashore," she said, "as long as we can get Shadrach off, too."

They pulled the gangplank almost to shore, but once again they had difficulty getting Shadrach to move. They went through the long process of pushing, pulling, coaxing, and bribing, until at last they got him splashing off the gangplank and wading onto dry land.

"Keep him moving, or he'll stop again!" Mikey called to Hannah, who was pulling on Shadrach's rope.

They took him along the stony beach until they found a flat area in bushes that looked good for shelter.

"Are we going to camp here?" Sky wanted to know.

"Don't ask me," said Hannah, who was suddenly very tired of having to make all the decisions.

"What are we going to do?" Mikey asked.

"You tell me," Hannah replied.

"Maybe no one will come after us," said Sky. "When the tide comes in, we can go home."

"That's just what I was thinking," said Hannah.

"What if someone does come?" Mikey asked.

"We'll stay hidden in the bushes," said Hannah.

"What then?" asked Mikey.

But no one had an answer to that.

CHAPTER THIRTEEN

Joe and Sophie didn't get anywhere with Craig Benny, the owner of the Wuff Stuff dog food factory. The man was so angry he was beyond reason. Sophie refunded his thirty dollars, but the man was demanding a large amount of money, which got larger as he went on—three thousand, four thousand, ten thousand.

"My business is ruined! My horses are all gone! They threatened my life! They pushed me in! I call that attempted murder!"

"How deep is the pond?" Sophie asked.

"That's not the point! I could die of salmonella or tetanus. If I got hold of those kids— Every horse in the place gone! Gone! I'll have to close the factory! I'll go bankrupt!"

"Why don't you have your horses back?" Joe asked. "Some of them must have been returned."

"Because they've all been stolen, that's why! You owe me a lot of money, mister!"

"You're sure you haven't seen the children since?" asked Joe.

"No, I haven't. And just as well for them. You're accountable. They're your kids! Or are you like the rest of modern parents? Raise a bunch of hooligans, no responsibility—"

"We'll be in touch, Mr. Benny," said Sophie. "Come on, Joe."

"What are you going to do about it?" the man yelled after them.

Back in the car, Joe said, "Phew! What a place! The smell is unbelievable!"

"So is the owner," said Sophie. "I wanted to push him right back into that filthy pond. I was so angry. Our children having to cope with that—that—"

"I think they looked after themselves all right," said Joe, grinning.

"It's not funny, Joe!" said Sophie. Then she burst out laughing.

Farther down the road, they pulled into a gas station. As the attendant cleaned their windshield, Joe said, "I don't suppose you've seen three children and an old draft horse in the area."

"Horses?" said the attendant. "Man, have I seen horses! All the old nags from the dog food factory—and could they move! Down this road lickety-split, and into town. Then things started happening. It was on the radio. People called in.

That factory's been operating illegally ever since Benny took over. So there was the health inspector and the people from the Society for the Protection of Animals. They took the horses away and closed the factory. What comings and goings!"

"This is just three children and a draft horse," said Joe. "Two boys and a girl."

The attendant shook his head. "Were they the ones who started it? No. I tell you, I kept an eye on what was going on, and I didn't see three youngsters. Your kids, are they?"

"I don't know whether to say yes or no," said Joe.

The attendant laughed. "They sure started something."

From the gas station, Sophie and Joe drove around the neighborhood, stopping at houses within a two-block radius, asking the same questions and getting the same answers. People had seen the horses. They'd heard about it on their radios. But it was as though Hannah, Mikey, Sky, and Shadrach had left the factory and dropped into a hole in the ground.

Joe said to Sophie, "Three children and a big horse that can barely walk don't disappear like that."

"They could have an adult working with them," said Sophie. "Someone with a horse trailer. Ask yourself, how did they get to Nelson in the first place? Do you think three children are capable of organizing an escapade like this?"

"Our three are," said Joe.

Sophie was silent. Then she said, "It'll be dark soon. They don't have coats. Sky gets croup in the night air."

Joe nodded. "We'll call Maree Gerritsen again. Maybe she's heard something. If she hasn't, we'd better contact the police."

Sophie nodded. "We've had no luck. I think it'll have to be a full-scale search."

They stopped at the next phone booth, and Sophie got out. Joe folded his arms on the steering wheel and rested his head on them, thinking, "Let them be okay. Keep them safe."

Sophie wasn't long. The way she opened the car door made Joe lift his head in hope. She was laughing, shaking, on the verge of tears. "They've been in Havelock. They hijacked a boat!"

"What?"

"They're fine, and Shadrach's with them. Three kids and a horse steaming out of Havelock on Wally Yates's mussel barge."

"The little monsters!" Joe began to laugh. He slapped the steering wheel as though he were playing drums and beat on the roof lining above his head. He called out, "Wow! Wow! Yeee-ow!" Then he leaned across, grabbed Sophie's face between his hands, and kissed her noisily.

Not far out of Nelson, Joe switched on the car's headlights. He was wondering how the children would get the mussel barge home in the dark.

Sophie was more concerned with the greater predicament. "I don't know what I'm going to say to Hannah," she said. "I won't be able to look her in the eye."

Joe shrugged. "It's not a good situation for parents to be in. A family pet is sick. It has to be put to sleep. What do you tell your kids, for heaven's sake?"

"It might have been better if we'd just shot him and buried him on the farm."

"That's probably what will happen. But who's going to shoot Shadrach? Who's going to dig the hole?" Joe looked at her. "You have first dibs."

Sophie sighed. "If I were Hannah, I think I could accept that. It's this business of making him into dog food. At the time it seemed like such a good idea. There was even something okay about getting money for him and putting it toward a new pony."

"We can't blame ourselves for doing what we thought was best," said Joe. "On the other hand, maybe we shouldn't have gone overboard with the Rest Home for Aged Equestrian Friends bit."

"We?" Sophie laughed. "Joe, why do you always insist on sharing my shortcomings? You mean me. I told them that story."

"And very believable it was, too," grinned Joe. "I could see it all clearly—clover paddocks with white picket fences, heated stables—and you tell me you're worried about Hannah's imagination!"

"Oh, Joe, don't!" winced Sophie. She slumped back in the seat. "What are we going to say to them?"

"For a start," said Joe, "I think we should say we're sorry."

Chapter Fourteen

The barge was afloat, and they could have continued their journey. The trouble now was Shadrach. He wouldn't get up. He just lay there among the grasses and driftwood, making snoring noises and frothing at the mouth. Mikey couldn't even get him to raise his head.

"Let him rest a few minutes," Hannah said. "He'll be all right."

"Why don't we go home and leave him," Mikey suggested. "We can come and get him in the morning."

"We're staying with him," Hannah said.

"It's dark. I'm hungry."

"You know what he's like," Hannah said. "He gets exhausted. Then he rests, and he's okay again."

"Well, I'm not okay. I'm freezing."

"Wait on the boat," said Hannah. "It'll be warmer."

But Mikey didn't move. He wrapped his arms around himself and tried to hug in what warmth he had left.

No one had come after them. Two boats had gone past, both out in the middle of the sound. They heard engines and saw the lights disappear. It was very dark now, except for a rim of green light over the western hills. Above them the stars were glittering like splintered glass. They had found shelter under some tree ferns, but the ground near them was already wet with dew.

Sky was shivering. He wanted to go back on the boat but not on his own.

"It won't be long and we'll all be back," said Hannah. "Come here, and I'll tell you a story."

"Hannibal Megosaurus?" asked Sky.

"You didn't say 'apricot.'"

"I keep on forgetting." Sky snuggled up to her and put his thumb in his mouth.

"It's very important, Sky—Boomy-boomy-nutcake. It's a magic formula. Hannibal Megosaurus is not too powerful for animals, because they are part of nature. But people need protection."

"Human beans," said Sky.

"Repeat after me: 'apricot, apricot, apricot.'"

Sky took his thumb out of his mouth. "I'm not Boomy-boomy-nutcake now. My new name is Apricot."

"It can't be!"

"Yes, it is."

"That would spoil the magic," Hannah said.

"I'm Apricot. I'm protected all the time. Go on with the story."

"Sky, I can't. You have to think of some other name."

"Not Sky. Apricot!"

Mikey interrupted. "Just for once, let's have a real story."

"They are real stories," said Hannah.

"I mean factual," Mikey said.

"Like what?"

"Things that really happen. You know, an earthquake or a shipwreck."

He wasn't trying to be smart, but Hannah reacted badly. "It's not wrecked! There's nothing wrong with it!"

"Don't you two ever stop fighting?" said Sky in a bored voice. "You said we could have a story."

"Mikey's telling it," said Hannah in a huffy voice.

"I can hear a boat coming," said Mikey.

There was a pause.

"Where?" said Sky. "What happens?"

"It's not a story," said Mikey, standing up. "A boat is really coming."

On the other side of the sound, a boat was traveling slowly. A strong finger of light touched the water in front and to either side. Back and forth it went, sweeping over the white hills.

"A searchlight!" Mikey cried. "They're looking for us!"

He ran down to the water's edge, waved his arms in the dark, and yelled, "Hey! We're here!"

"Mikey!" Hannah came after him. "Stop that! They'll see you!"

"I want them to!" cried Mikey. "I want to go home!"

But the boat was far away, and the beam of light missed them. The boat went past, and the sound of its engine grew quieter with the distance.

Mikey began to cry.

"We are going home," Hannah said, "just as soon as Shadrach's ready to walk."

"I want to go home now."

"Oh, Mikey, I get tired of explaining things to you. You're so stubborn."

"I'm not stubborn. You're the stubborn one!"

The wake from the boat broke in waves against the shore beside them. Far away, they could still see the light moving like a thin, white pencil, but they could no longer hear the engine.

Hannah was standing beside Mikey. Suddenly she jumped as though she'd been stung by something. "Shadrach's gone!" she said.

Mikey turned. He couldn't see anything but was aware that the snoring noise had stopped.

"He couldn't be gone," he said.

"He is! He is!" said Hannah in a quick, high voice. "He's gone away! I can feel it!"

"No," called Sky somewhere in front of them. "He's still here."

"Gone," repeated Hannah, not moving.

Mikey stumbled through the grass to the place where Shadrach was lying. He squatted down and touched the horse's head, his neck, his chest. "He's not breathing," he said.

Sky called back to Hannah, "Shadrach's not breathing!"

Hannah took a few steps toward them and stopped.

Mikey ran his hands over the horse's coat. It was warm and floppy as though the muscle under it had melted. He could pick up a handful of skin and hair like loose clothing.

"We could breathe in his mouth," Sky suggested.

Mikey put his hand against Shadrach's mouth and nose, which were still wet with froth and warm. Nothing moved. In the dark, his hand went over the horse's whiskers, up the bone of his face to his mane and ears. He then wiped his hand on his shorts and looked back for Hannah. He could barely see her. "Hannah? I think Shadrach's dead."

Sky began to weep, but there was no sound from Hannah.

"Hannah?" Mikey said.

Then a strong, white beam fell on them like sudden daylight.

Mikey clearly saw Shadrach's head stretched back, the mouth open and the eyes sunk deep. He saw Sky with his fists against his eyes, and farther back, Hannah standing still, staring.

The boat had turned back and was coming toward them. People were shouting. He recognized the voices, but now he was unable to call out.

"Hannah? Mikey? Sky?" Joe was calling.

As the boat neared them, there was a splash. Sophie was over the side in water up to her waist, wading ashore. And then Hannah was running, down to the sound and in, still trying to run, lurching, arms out to Sophie. And they were in the water together holding each other tight, and Hannah was crying against Sophie as though she would never stop.

CHAPTER FIFTEEN

They had the funeral late the following afternoon in heavy rain.

Wally Yates winched Shadrach aboard his mussel barge and brought him home. Joe had the tractor and trailer ready on the beach to take him the rest of the way to the paddock. That morning, the road maintenance man Aldwyn Smith had found someone in the area with a backhoe, and by half-past four the hole was ready. Shadrach lay in it with his head on his old blanket and a garland of flowers around his neck.

Most of the children from the Waitaria Bay school came. So did Mr. and Mrs. Gerritsen, Mr. and Mrs. Smith, and Miss McNicol, who all lived near the school.

They thought the rain might hold off, but heavy drops started as everyone arrived. By the time the funeral service started, there was a steady downpour, with water streaming down jackets, raincoats, and umbrellas. The dirt at their feet turned to a yellow paste that clung in thick lumps to their rain boots.

Joe began the service by talking about love. He said that love made things immortal, and nothing ever died if it was loved. Then he talked about Shadrach.

"He gave us his love. We gave him ours. And because love is a gift of oneself, Shadrach wasn't just a horse. He was us. He was family. But especially he was Hannah, because she loved him the most."

Sophie said that Shadrach had taught her some very important things about truth and justice. She told everyone how proud she was of Hannah and Mikey and Sky for having the courage to do what they believed was right.

"If it hadn't been for Shadrach," said Mrs. Gerritsen, "there would be no news on the front page of this morning's Nelson paper. My mother tells me there's a big photo of runaway horses in a coffee shop."

Mr. Gerritsen said his strongest memory of Shadrach was of this huge horse shuffling along the road to school with two little children on his back.

Wally Yates laughed. "I remember that! I saw them a couple of times. He was the ugliest horse ever. It was an honor to bring him home for the last time."

Mikey said he would always remember how clever Shadrach was and all the circus tricks he'd been able to do.

"Like bowing down," said Sky.

"I saw Shadrach bow down," said Eliana Grouse, who was standing next to Hannah and holding an umbrella over her.

"He bowed down for the Wuff Stuff man," grinned Sky.

One at a time, they all said something about Shadrach—all except Hannah. Joe looked at her and raised his eyebrows a little, but she shook her head.

Miss McNicol, who had brought a basket of flowers from her garden, passed them around and suggested that each person throw a flower into the grave with a loving thought of Shadrach.

When that was done, they went back to the house, dropped their coats and boots on the porch, and sat inside eating scones with cream and raspberry jam. Mr. Smith's friend stayed behind at the grave, filling the hole with his backhoe.

The rain was heavy all night, and the next day and night as well. Mist hung over the hills, and the flat, gray sea was patterned with dancing circles. Everything shone with wetness: bush grass, stones, house, sheds, the raw earth of the grave. In most paddocks, new little streams ran down the creases of the land, while the creek that gave the farm its water supply flooded to roaring rapids that broke their banks.

When the rain finally stopped, Hannah went up the thundering creek to look at the sacred place. The square rock that had been the throne of Hannibal Megosaurus was almost under water. The bones were gone.

CHAPTER SIXTEEN

Through summer, autumn, and winter, the children found flowers to put on Shadrach's grave, but by late the next spring, the grave was growing flowers of its own. From the bare earth sprouted the soft green of foxglove plants, and then the stems produced rows of purple buds.

Hannah said it was a miracle that foxgloves should be growing there and not in the rest of the paddock. Sophie pointed out that when the earth was laid bare, the first plants to grow in it were always foxgloves and bracken fern.

During that spring, Hannah went on a pony ride with her friends Debbie, Kirsty, and Eliana. Hannah rode a horse she borrowed from Mrs. Gerritsen. Sophie thought that it might be time to talk again about a new pony.

"No thanks," said Hannah.

"Is this answer for yourself? Or have you consulted the others?" said Sophie. "Sky and Mikey might like to have a horse."

"I don't mind," said Mikey. "I'd rather have a mountain bike."

"We don't have that kind of money," said Sophie.

"A skateboard would be okay," Mikey suggested.

"Two skateboards!" put in Sky.

"Where would you go with a skateboard?" Sophie asked.

They thought about that. "Our room?" Sky suggested.

"What about an outboard motor for our dinghy?" Mikey said.

Sophie threw her hands up. "Mikey, I'm not asking for your Christmas present list. I merely wondered if it was time we got a horse. We've always had one around the place."

"It isn't," said Hannah.

"Isn't what?"

"Isn't time."

"Look at it this way, Sophie," said Mikey. "If one of us died and people said you should adopt a child—"

"All right! All right! I've got the message! I won't mention it again."

"I still wouldn't mind a skateboard," Sky said.

"Ask the old man who comes down the chimney," Sophie replied.

The previous Christmas, Hannah's present had been a thick, blank writing book for her stories, but she still preferred telling them aloud to Mikey and Sky at night after the light was out. Stories always grew well in darkness. Hannibal Megosaurus had been gone for some time. Now there was Fire-eater, a huge horse who lived among the stars and who came to earth like Superman to rescue children from extreme hardship and danger. Hannah did try writing some of this in her book, but she found that writing somehow made her stories heavy and dull. A talking voice had expression. It could laugh or sound scary. And it wasn't full of smudges and words crossed out. She explained that to Sophie and asked if she could use the book as a photo album.

It was Joe who took most of the photos in the family. On the night of Sky's sixth birthday party, he put his camera on a tripod and took pictures of Sky blowing out candles on the cake Mikey had made him, and more pictures of him opening his presents. There was a T-shirt from Sophie and Joe, a glove puppet made by Hannah, Mikey's extra chess set, which Sky kept borrowing anyway, and a bunch of foxgloves from Shadrach.

Joe was about to take a photo of the cake being cut when the phone rang. He went out to the kitchen to answer it and was gone so long that Sky cut the cake anyway. They were having seconds when Joe came back.

He came in hopping from one foot to the other and snapping his fingers, although there was no music playing. His face was carefully blank, but they knew he was excited about something.

Sophie decided that she wouldn't ask him about the phone call, but Hannah and Mikey, who were keenly sensitive to their father's moods, did.

"Oh, just a friend," said Joe.

"What friend?" Hannah asked.

"Someone I've known for years." Joe took a bite of cake and then suddenly laughed, spluttering crumbs.

"What's up?" Mikey asked.

"Do we know who it is?" said Hannah.

"Matter of fact, you do. You saw him last year. Nigel Stack."

"Oh—him!" Hannah said.

"That's the man who took Shadrach away," said Sky. "He works for the racehorse place in Christchurch."

"Not any more, he doesn't. Got himself a new job. Mikey, this cake is delicious. You can make it for me any time. Don't have to wait for my birthday."

"What has cake got to do with Nigel Stack?" asked Mikey.

"Nothing," said Joe. "I was giving you a well-earned compliment."

"What did Nigel Stack say?" Mikey persisted.

"A lot. A very great deal."

"Are you going to tell us, or aren't you?" said Sophie, losing patience with his game.

"Tell you what?" Joe looked at her with innocent eyes.

She decided to ignore him by stacking the dishes and carrying them toward the kitchen.

"Wait!" said Joe. "Don't you want to hear? Nigel got fired. But he's found another job on the North Island. Much better, he said. On the way, he's going to stop and see us."

"That's nice," said Sophie.

"Big deal!" said Sky.

And Hannah said nothing.

"Is that all?" Mikey asked.

"You know why he was fired?" said Joe, leaning across the table. "Because of us."

"For coming here?" said Sophie. "That's a bit harsh, isn't it?"

Joe nodded. "You remember he had a champion mare, Lacemaker? He was supposed to take her directly to Nelson."

"He was only a day late," Sophie said. "He could have broken an axle anywhere."

Joe wiped his hand over his face. "The trouble is, Lacemaker has recently foaled. Nigel says it's the ugliest little filly he's ever seen, with big hooves and head, and an over-developed jaw. Part thoroughbred, part Clydesdale. Nigel got fired and was told to destroy the foal. He didn't. He found another mother for it, and it's been doing very well." Joe looked from face to face around the table and finished up grinning at Hannah. "Does anyone want another horse?"